These Niggas Ain't Loyal 2

Nikki Tee

**Lock Down Publications
Presents
These Niggas Ain't Loyal 2
A Novel by *Nikki Tee***

Lock Down Publications
P.O. Box 1482
Pine Lake, Ga 30072-1482

Lock Down Publications
Like our page on Facebook: Lock Down Publications
@www.facebook.com/lockdownpublications.ldp
Facebook: Author Nikki Tee
Email: msnikkit504@gmail.com
Cover design and layout by: Dynasty Cover Me
Book interior design by: Shawn Walker
Edited by: Tumika Cain

DEDICATION

This book is dedicated to all the women who have been in Shaunie's shoes. No matter the race, religion, or economic class, there is a woman who had faced this heart break and pain. This is someone's story. Women, by nature, are loyal to those we love. When we love, we love with our whole heart and without reservation. Only a pain so deep and profound can cause us to sever the bonds that anchor us to whom we have given our loyalty to. My hope is that you keep moving forward, in spite of your pain, and don't let what you have been through define you.

ACKNOWLEDGEMENT

I owe thanks to so many people, but first I have to thank the man above who blessed me and allowed me to write this story.

My family, friends, and avid readers are the cornerstone for the success of my work and inspiration for me to continue to write. To all of you, thank you for all of the support you have given me. Many readers contacted me and told me how much they loved the story and how they went through something similar. Thank you all for the support. I hope you are able to take something away from the many messages that are ingrained in the story.

I want to thank my sister Robin Torregano for being a test reader and encouraging me when I doubted myself. I love you.

The women of *Coffee's Lounge* are the bomb. You ladies are an amazing group of people. I am blessed to be a part of such a warm, loving, crazy group. Our discussions put a smile on my face on some of my gloomiest days. I have never been the type of person to call people who aren't related to me by blood, sister, but I learned that not all sisters are sisters by blood but by heart. My sisters of the lounge Rocks!

SWP (Sisters with Pen Game), I have always had an affinity for strong black women who are constantly striving to be success and support each other. You ladies have welcomed me with open arms. I'm so grateful to have gotten a chance to know you all. Let's continue to grow together.

To the women of *JPeach Spot,* you know who you are so I will not list names. I have never met a nuttier group of women. Words can't describe y'all. You all are very expressive, comically, loyal, and supportive. I got many request from y'all on how Keyz should die a slow agonizing death. Y'all act like this is real. Oh hell, who am I kidding. I am always right there with y'all fussing and getting mad! I couldn't have gotten a more loyal and supportive group to be a part of.

Notes: Please take a moment to show your support by leaving a review.

Nikki Tee

Chapter 1

Loyalty is a funny thing. So was love. They both hit you when you least expect it.

—*Jodi Lynn Anderson*

Keyz

I walked to the area that had been cleared for the funeral service, noting with approval that the funeral director followed my instructions for the arrangements to the tee. Ten feet from the grave, a white gazebo was set up with chairs covered with pink linen. On each chair was a single pink rose.

Taking my time, I turned to face the grave and the casket. *Man, this shit hurts,* I thought as I wrestled with my emotional and mental anguish to keep a calm exterior. The memory of the day the doctor came out to the waiting room and told me she didn't make it will forever be ingrained in my mind, heart, and soul. When the doctor approached me with the facial expression that he came bearing sad news, my heart dropped to my stomach. Before he could deliver the news, I broke down crying in the waiting room. I felt such hopelessness, all I could do was cry. That one moment brought me, my family, and friends here today.

A lone tear fell from my eyes as the pain caused my chest to hurt and my eyes to water. Her life was cut short all because of my secrets and lies caught up to me. I removed my shades and quickly wiped the tear away with the back of my hand before I pinched the bridge of my nose to help me get my composure.

My feet took small, measured steps as I walked towards the area that would be the final resting place of my beloved. Stopping in front of the casket, I kept my head up so as not to look at the casket first. I thought about the customized headstone I ordered. The bronze headstone had angel wings on each side. The angel wings were sculptured to appear to swoop down. In the cradle of the wings, was a being with a halo around her head. The angels came to claim one of their own. At the bottom of the headstone was a family of three watching their loved one being taken up to heaven. To complete the design, in the middle was an epitaph dedicated to the deceased. I knew the headstone engraver was going to do a remarkable job designing the headstone capturing the intricate design I demanded, because he was the best in the area and I doubled his price as the guarantee of a superb end product.

Once I was done visualizing the headstone, I finally built up enough courage to look at the casket. I placed my trembling hand on the smooth surface. The casket was pink with gold trim. It was beautiful. The angel that was inside of it was beautiful, too. *This wasn't how it was supposed to be*, I thought. I stood in front of the casket and thought about the should haves, could haves, and would haves.

"Come on, baby, the pastor is ready to start the service," my mama said as she walked up to me and patted my back. I turned around and looked at the sea of faces staring back at me. Everyone had somber expressions on their faces for this solemn event. I looked at Ms. Sharon sitting in the front row trying to comfort Keira, who was sitting in her lap. Keira didn't understand where her Mommy was. Seeing my baby girl crying, asking for her mom caused me to freeze in place, as the scene of finding the love of my life unresponsive in the tub played before my eyes, like the event had just taken place only yesterday.

Shaunie was in the tub leaning back with her eyes closed. I told her over and over again about that shit. She loved to relax in the tub and almost always started to fall asleep. I leaned over the tub and touched her beautiful face. She looked so peaceful. I hated to wake her up.

"Wake up, ma." Shaunie didn't stir, so I gently shook her. Her head slumped back to the side. It was then that I finally noticed the Ciroc bottle in the tub and the pill bottle on the floor.

"Shhhhaaaunnie, noooo!"

The thought of her destroying herself was too much for me to bear. "No, No, No," I repeated like a mantra as I grabbed her out of the tub and rocked her back and forth, willing her to open her eyes. Tears were falling uncontrollably out of my eyes. Her skin was warm to the touch and that gave me hope. I didn't feel the rise and fall of her chest.

"Oh, fuck! Baby, hang on. I'm so sorry. Please, just please." I pulled out my cell to call for help.

My hands shook as I dialed 911.

"What's your emergency?" the operator asked.

"I need an ambulance, my fiancée isn't breathing. I think she OD'd."

A loud sob made me come back to the present. To my left, Thugga was holding Nikki in his arms as she tried to cry quietly. Several other people were trying to hold back their cries, while others quietly sniffled.

I sat in my chair in between my mama and Ms. Sharon. "It's going to be okay, Keyon. God called home an angel. That angel served her purpose and now it's time for her to go back to paradise." She grabbed my hand in hers. It felt so good to get comfort from my mama. She aggravates me sometimes with all the fussing and nagging she does, but whenever I needed her, she was always there for me. I nodded my head to let her know I heard her.

"Ahem." The pastor cleared his throat to get everyone's attention. "Thank you, everyone, for coming to this glorious home-going celebration. My thoughts and prayers have been nonstop since the unfortunate death of God's child. Many times, when we lose a loved one, we question God, asking why and how. Because we are human, he allows these questions. Death is part of the higher plan that a higher power has for us. It is with great sadness that one so young, who hasn't even experienced life is gone. Matthew 5 verse 4 says 'Blessed are those who mourn, for they will be comforted.' May all of you family and friends of our dearly departed receive that comfort in the days ahead."

After the pastor finished his sermon, the singer that was hired sung *Borrowed Angels* by Kristin Chenoweth. The lyrics had even the hardest gangsta present crying. Today was a reminder to everyone there that what can be here today, can be gone tomorrow.

Chapter 2

Loyalty is sometimes so resplendent as to make a man walk through life amid glory and acclamation; but it burns very dimly and low when carried into "the valley of the shadow of death."

-W. Mountford

Shaunie

My body felt lethargic. I couldn't move, no matter how hard I tried. Maybe it was the numbness that was spreading up my legs towards the rest of my body that prevented movement. I tried several times to open my eyes, but they remained closed. They felt as if they were glued stuck with something permanent.

Someone was calling my name and shaking me, telling me to wake up. That voice sounded familiar to me, but I was so confused and couldn't place it. I wanted to answer them, but just couldn't. Hands were on my body, but it seemed to be from a distance. Everything and every sensation started to slow down and fade into the background. The person calling my name was now calling from a distance.

An earthquake shook my body as I lost complete control of my movements. As I faded in and out of awareness of my surroundings, I felt myself being pulled towards something, but I couldn't tell what. Someone pressed something into my mouth. Willing myself to move, I tried to turn my head away, but didn't have the strength to fight. My heart rate slowed down until there was just a thump every few seconds. "Code Blue!" I heard someone yell as my heart beat stopped. God, I am so tired, was my last thought before I gave in to the darkness that besieged me.

Waking up with a jolt, I noticed I was lying in the grass. I picked myself up and looked around in confusion. *Where am I?* I was in a meadow of grass. The grass was the most vibrant shade I had ever seen, having an incorporeal feel when I bent down to touch it. Even though I felt it, I didn't truly feel it. *How did I get here?* Spinning around in a circle, I tried to take everything in. *Am I dreaming?* Pillows of white clouds that floated all around surrounded me. I felt a thought in my head pushing towards the forefront of my mind, but it was just out of reach. Confusion was now my companion. I didn't know if I was dreaming or how I got to this strange place. One of the clouds nudged me as it floated by. Everything felt so real.

"Hey, baby girl." That voice had greeted me with those same words for twenty-two years. The caress of that voice made me feel safe. I felt at home.

Turning around, I faced my daddy for the first time in two years. He looked the same as I remembered. "Oh my god, daddy," I said as I launched myself into his arms, holding on and never wanting to let go. Pulling back, I re-familiarized myself with his face. "I've missed you so much." Tears of joy filled my eyes, because I never thought I would see him again. I raised my hand to wipe away the tears, but there weren't any. It felt like I was crying, but there was no evidence.

Then it hit me like a freight train. My dad died two years ago. That meant I was with him in a place away from the rest of my family. I put my hand to my mouth and gasped.

"Daddy, what happened to me?" I started to look around in panic. I didn't remember what events took place for me to find myself here. My dad looked at me with a strange expression on his face. I tried to decipher the look, but the expression was quickly replaced with one of calming.

"Now don't you worry, baby girl. Calm down. The time to explain that will come. I have two very special people who are anxious to meet you," he said. He looked behind him. From behind my dad materialized a little boy holding an infant swaddled in a pink gown. My dad took the bundle from the little boy's arms.

Slowly, I walked towards the little boy who was a replica of Keyz. I stared in awe when he smiled at me, feeling my heart reach out to him and invisible threads linking us together. I felt a closeness to this child that could only be from the bonds of mother and child.

"You are as pretty up close as you are from afar," the little boy said to me. He had a twinkle in his dark brown eyes.

I reached my hand out and stroked the side of his face. My mind told me he was my child, but I couldn't comprehend it.

"Who are you?" I asked him as I continued to stroke his face. He placed his hand over mine and I felt a completion I had never felt before.

"I'm KJ and I'm six years old." He smiled up at me. This was my baby, the first child that was placed in my womb that I didn't carry due to a bad decision that I regretted every day.

Looking back at him, I wished that things could have been different. I wanted to tell him how I regretted my decision, how I cried every night for a year, and how I longed to hold him in my arms, but knew I never could. "I'm so sorry," was all I was able to croak out.

He wrapped his arms around my legs. He didn't say anything to my apology. I reached down and lifted him in my arms. He laid his head on my shoulder and I laid my head on top of his. I felt at peace.

A low wail interrupted my reunion with KJ. I was so caught up in my shock, I forgot about the bundle wrapped in pink. I walked towards my dad with KJ still in my arms.

"Someone wants to meet you," my dad said. He cradled the bundle in his arms and outstretched them towards me.

I looked down and stared at a mirror image of myself.

"She's beautiful," I said. The baby smiled at me. I put KJ down and took the baby from my dad's arms. I knew she was mine, but I didn't know how. This place had me so confused. The baby nuzzled my chest as she snuggled closer into me. I lifted her up as I bent my head and placed a kiss to her cupid bow shaped lips.

"Daddy named her Keyshaun," KJ informed me. "She came here with me, because she came too early. Grandpa said I have to take care of my baby sister." He puffed his little chest out.

I felt pride surge through me for my son. What a great protector he was for Keyshaun and would have been for Keira.

"Well, I'm here now so we can take care of her together." I rocked my daughter in my arms. My dad walked up to KJ and placed his hand on his shoulder.

"Shaunie, you are not here for long, baby girl. You will have to leave soon." The thought of leaving my kids and the peacefulness I felt caused a moment of panic.

It seemed cruel to experience this moment when it wasn't meant to last. "Why? Why am I here if I can't stay with y'all?" I asked my dad. I wanted to be angry that I would have to leave them so soon, but this place wouldn't let me succumb to any negative feelings.

"I don't know the answer to that, but I do know it isn't your time. The time will come when we will all be reunited, but this isn't it." He reached for Keyshaun. I reluctantly handed her to him. "I'll take very good care of them until the time comes for you to join them. It's time to say goodbye now."

I nodded my head. I didn't know if I wanted to go back. The tranquility here was everything I needed. I got down on a knee in front of KJ, memorizing his face until the day I saw him again.

"I love you," I whispered to him before I pulled him into an embrace. Seeing and holding my son made me feel a whole in a way that I hadn't been in a long time. The void inside of me that I carried around for so long felt like it was finally being filled with closure. All the could haves and should haves that I secretly asked myself whenever I thought of that abortion, was washed away.

"I love you too, mama. Don't be sad. I'll see you again."

Not wanting to let go, I pulled back and placed a kissed on his forehead.

I stood up and walked to my dad. I hugged him with the baby between us. "Bye, daddy. I love you. Mom misses you every day." I pulled back from him and took my baby from him. "I love you too, little one. I'm sorry." I choked out. I kissed her once again and gave her to my dad. I didn't want to leave, but I felt something pulling me in a vortex.

"Don't fight it, baby girl. It's taking you where you belong." I struggled against the pull. I didn't want to leave. The familiar had become the unknown and I wasn't ready to face whatever it was. I fought against the pull until once again, I succumbed to the darkness.

Chapter 3

Loyalty is like love. Anybody can say they have it but only the real live it and show it.

-Unknown

Keyz

After making sure my baby girl was laid to rest, I spent every moment in the hospital with Shaunie. I was fucked up about the baby. Shaunie was four and a half months pregnant when she overdosed. Due to stress, the medication, and alcohol, the baby couldn't handle the strain. Shortly after I arrived at the hospital, Shaunie slipped into a coma. The doctor informed me that Shaunie was pregnant. I knew she didn't know she was pregnant, because she had been taking birth control pills until the day when she found out about Shaun three weeks ago.

When the doctors told me about the baby and the likelihood of a miscarriage, I prayed to God like I'd never prayed before. I didn't want Shaunie to go through the loss of another child. She barely kept it together when she had the abortion. The baby didn't make it through the night. She miscarried the baby and the doctor had to perform a D&C to remove the rest of our baby's remains. They wanted to dispose of the remains, but I said fuck that. That's my seed and she deserved a proper burial.

I made the doctor tell me everything about the fetus. He looked at me like I was crazy. He advised me to seek counseling. I told him if he didn't tell me what I wanted to know, he would need physical therapy after I break his legs. He told me it was a girl and the baby was practically fully developed and was about four and a half inches. I tried to wait for Shaunie to come out of the coma so we could do the memorial service together, but she stayed in a coma for two weeks. I thought something was wrong, but the doctors assured me her body just needed the rest.

The sound of the door opening caused me to look up and see Ms. Sharon walking in. After the incident, I was worried that Shaunie's mom would blame me for everything that happened, but surprisingly, she didn't blame me for what she deemed was an accident. I sat up when she walked in the room.

"Good morning, Keyon, have there been any changes?" She sat in the other chair next to Shaunie's bed. Pulling Shaunie's hand in hers, she tucked the covers over her daughter.

I shook my head. "Good morning. The doctors said she will come around when her body is ready to wake up."

"Honey, why don't you go downstairs and get yourself something to eat. You are not going to do anybody any good if you are not healthy yourself. You still have Keira to look after." She paused. "And Shaunie," she said looking my in the eyes. I looked back at her searching for anger. I knew I would be angry if a nigga stepped out on my daughter and had a child with someone else. All I saw in her eyes was disappointment.

I broke eye contact with her and stood up. I had enough to deal with without adding more disappointment to my ever growing list of fuck ups. "Imma head to the cafeteria and get a bit to eat. You want something?"

"No, I'm fine. Thank you." She turned back to Shaunie and stroked her face. I looked at my wifey before I walked out the door. I hoped she woke up soon. We had a lot to talk about and this distance between us was stressing me out. I had been on my way to her house to try and resolve our issues when I found her unconscious, so we never had a chance to talk. The stress I had felt then, had only mounted since that time.

I went to the cafeteria and ordered something to eat. Food was the farthest thing on my mind and I had no appetite. I was just going through the motions. My cell phone began to vibrate. I

Nikki Tee

pulled it out and looked at the name. "Fuck she want," I muttered. "What up?" I asked when I answered the call.

I heard teeth smacking through the phone. "Is that any way to answer the phone when the mother of your son calls?" Ashley asked me. This bitch was a thorn in my side that I had been forced to deal with since she trapped me with my son. Our relationship was constantly strained, because she wanted to act like we were a family or some shit, when all I wanted to do was take care of my kid. She act like I trapped her and not the other way around.

"I ain't got no time for all that bullshit. What do you want?"

"Your son has been asking about you. When are you coming over to spend time with him?"

"I don't know. I been busy." No need to tell her what's been up.

"Yeah, I heard that weak bitch of yours tried to off herself," Ashley said, laughing.

My hand gripped the phone tighter. This bitch was really testing me. I guess that ass whipping wasn't enough after she showed up to Shaunie's job causing a scene trying to get her fired. My wifey beat her ass and sent her on her way with a fucked up, bloody face.

26

"Bitch, I told ya ass about playing with her. Ain't shit weak about my girl. You know what? Imma see you." I hung up in her face. I was gon' beat the fuck out of her ass when I saw her. Ain't shit funny about me and Shaunie's situation. These side hoes really be getting mad at the main chick. That shit stupid. This bitch got me wondering how she even knew about Shaunie being in the hospital. I knew for a fact her and Shaunie didn't run in the same circles, because if that was the case, Shaunie would have been found out about Shaun. Somebody I knew been talking with Ashley's hoe ass.

It didn't matter though. Hoes like Ashley understood only one thing. Money. Imma cut off the money train and see what that hoe had to say then. I dumped my food and headed back to Shaunie's room to be with my baby. I walked in the room and saw Shaunie's mom watching TV. She looked at me and shook her head letting me know there had been no changes. I took my seat in the same spot I'd been in for the past few weeks. Since Shaunie was admitted, the only time I left the the hospital was to arrange and attend the memorial. I shaved, showered, and shitted at the hospital in Shaunie's room.

I'd started to drift off when I felt a twitch that came from the bed. Looking up, I came face to face with Shaunie's slanted hazel eyes. My own eyes got teary. Relief so profound overwhelmed me, it took me a minute to think about alerting her mom and the doctors. I didn't talk to God much, but with my eyes raised heavenward, I thanked him for allowing her to pull through.

"Ms. Sharon, she's up," I told her. I pressed the nurse call button and told them Shaunie was awake.

She jumped from her seat and came closer to the bed. "Oh thank you, Jesus! My baby is up. Shaunie, baby we were so worried. I'm so glad that you are going to be fine," she said in one breath. She had tears of relief falling from her eyes.

"Keira," Shaunie rasped. Her throat was sore and voice hoarse from disuse. She tried to swallow, but her throat was dry. Instead, her tongue darted out to moisten her lips.

"She's good, bae. My mama been taking care of her. She good, don't worry about that. Let's worry about getting you healthy, so you can come home," I told Shaunie. I lifted her hand and gave it a squeezed. Shaunie opened her mouth to say something, but the doctor interrupted when he came in.

The doctor walked up to the bed and checked her vitals. While the doctor told Shaunie what happened, she kept her eyes on me the entire time. When the doctor informed her about the miscarriage, her eyes brimmed with tears. Still, she didn't blink or break eye contact with me. My mind raced as I wondered what she was thinking and feeling. I wanted her to talk to me, but knew not to push her.

Once the doctor left after informing us that she could be released in a few days, Shaunie's mom stepped out to give us some privacy.

"I hate you" were the first words she said after almost three weeks of silence. Hearing those words from her was like a thousand bullets to my soul. My head was all fucked up. I knew she was all in her feelings and didn't mean that reckless shit, so I let it slide. I wanted things between us to be like it was before, but I didn't know if they could ever be that way again. On the real though, I knew it was my bad decisions and choices that led us here. In that moment, I hated myself, too.

Nikki Tee

Chapter 4

Show me disloyalty and I'll show you detachment.

-Unknown

Shaunie

It had been two weeks since I'd been released from the hospital. All I've done since then was lay around my mom's house watching TV and playing with Keira. I didn't answer calls from anyone. Keyz had been coming over every day to try and talk to me, but I remained quiet because there was nothing to say to that nigga. Everything heartbreaking and tragic that happened was on him and that's where the blame lay. When I woke up in the hospital from the coma and the doctors informed me of the miscarriage, a fire of hate raged in me. I thought it was a dream when I saw my dad and two babies. I didn't even know I was pregnant, but remembered being nauseous a few times. My situation with Keyz had me all over the place emotionally, physically, and mentally. I attributed it to being stressed.

I heard by mom coming down the stairs with a giggling Keira. Hearing her laughter made me think of happier times. The sound of

31

her laughing usually brought a smile to my face and lifted my spirits, but I was having a hard time shaking off the depression. What I wouldn't give to be so carefree and full of innocence like her.

"Keira and I are going to the store to buy some groceries. Do you need anything?" my mom asked me. She stood over the sofa in front of me with my baby on her hip.

I didn't even bother picking my head up off the pillow. "No, I'm fine," I said, still staring at the TV.

"You need to get up and shower. You have been in that same spot for days. Now, I tried to hold my peace and not say anything, but I have had enough. I am not going to sit back any longer and allow you to continue like this. I know you are hurting and you have every right to be, but at the same time, life goes on. You have a child to look after," she said in a matter-of-fact tone that let me know she meant business.

I looked up at her holding Keira. This depression was really hard to shake. It had such a hold on me that I barely did anything at all with Keira. Every time I felt ready to get up and moving so I could be a better mom, I got engulfed with feelings of hopelessness.

"I'm really trying, mom," I whined in a voice that I hardly recognized.

"Well, try harder. I know you are hurt, but don't sit here and let no man break you. It's time to get up."

Her words brought on a fresh batch of tears. "How could I be so stupid, mom? How could I have been so blind to what he had been doing behind my back?"

My mom sat on the sofa next to me and held me in her arms with Keira on her lap. "Baby, you weren't stupid, just inexperienced. How could you have known? You had never been with anyone before, least of all anyone like Keyz. Your relationship with him was your first and only. You gave him your trust and he didn't cherish it. We women are wired to love and when we love, we give our all. We never think that the one we love would mistreat us or abuse what we give them."

"Surely, there were signs. I was so weak for him," I said with disgust in my voice. That disgust was directed at myself. I allowed my love for a man overshadow the love for myself.

"Now you listen and listen good. No one is born strong. We all have to learn that characteristic. Situations and circumstances make people strong. What had you been through before this? Nothing! You had never been through anything before to test your

33

strength. There isn't woman alive who hasn't been super stupid for a man before. Trust and believe, we all have a story to tell. It's not about what you been through, but how you deal with the aftermath later. Where you were once weak, now is the time to find your strength and deal with the curveball life threw at you."

I turned to my mom and let my love and appreciation reflect in my eyes. "Okay, I'm getting up now," I told her with a small smile as I got up off the couch, placed a kissed to my baby's cheek and headed up the stairs. When I got to the bathroom, I turned the shower on hot, stripped out of my clothes and stepped under the water. As the water cascaded over my body, my tears began to fall.

I was on an emotional rollercoaster. Everything that went wrong in my life came to the forefront of my mind. The loss of my dad, the man who made everything better for me with just a few words and a hug. I thought I was coming to terms with the loss of my kids, but I cried for them, too.

My tears mingled with the water and the water washed them away. Falling to my knees, I curled myself in the fetal position and let out an unconstrained sob as all the hurt and pain was purged from my body and soul.

"*Why?!*" I screamed. My sobs and screams where muffled by the shower. Since no one was home, I allowed myself to indulge in my pity party. *This is the last time I will cry over this nigga and everything that had happened*, I told myself. Despite everything that happened with Keyz, from the cheating to the child, I had to acknowledge that he was good to me. He treated me like a queen and he made feel like the only woman alive when I was with him. But at this point how good he was to me wasn't enough to make up for the lies, deceit and betrayal.

I slipped on some shorts and a t-shirt without putting on a bra. My breasts were still sensitive from being engorged after the miscarriage. After putting my hair in a messy bun, I went downstairs, feeling much better after my cry session. I guess what they say was true: what soap is for the body, tears are for the soul. I felt rejuvenated. All that crying worked up an appetite, so I went in the kitchen to munch out.

Ding Dong.

The doorbell rang while I was stuffing my face with my mom's homemade sweet potato pie. I hadn't been able to eat much since I woke up from to the coma, so I was taking advantage of my appetite and eating nonstop.

"I'm coming," I yelled out, licking the spoon clean and headed to answer the door.

I came face to face with Keyz, yet again. Rolling my eyes, I allowed the venom to drip from my tone.

"What?" I asked him, leaving out pleasantries. This fool kept coming around trying to talk. He ain't have shit to say when he was fucking all those silicone pumped, black Barbie looking bitches, so he can save all that other shit for someone who gave a fuck. "Keira is gone with my mom."

"I know. I called your mama and she told me she was leaving to go get groceries. We need to talk," he said, pushing pass me and walking through the door.

I followed him to the living room. "We don't have shit to talk about. The time for talking is over." I folded my arms across my chest. The action lifted my breasts up. Keyz' eyes dropped down to my chest.

He quickly looked up with his lust-filled eyes. I saw love too, but I ignored that emotion. Love should have made his ass stay faithful the past seven years. His hands clenched at his side, like he was trying to suppress himself from grabbing and holding onto me. I smirked at him, thinking, *Yeah, get an eye full. That's all your ass is getting from me.* Keyz sighed, running his hands down his face. "When you gon' stop all this childish ass sulking and come your ass home? A nigga done apologized a million times." Frustration and regret lined every feature of his face.

My eyes almost bulged out my head. The nerve of this nigga. No the fuck he didn't stroll in my mom's house like the fucking king of the jungle, talking about apologies and coming home.

"I don't care how many times you apologized, it isn't going to change shit. That lame ass apology ain't gon' to erase all your fuck ups. It ain't gon' to bring my baby back either," I choked out. "I am not coming home, ever."

"I know you are hurt and in your feelings, but we ain't gon' resolve shit if we don't talk about it."

"In my feelings? Boy, you better shut up while you are ahead."

"Let's go to counseling."

I closed my eyes and prayed for patience. *Dear Lord, give me the strength to resist the temptation of murdering the dumbass in front of me.* "You know what? I am not trying to hear anything you have to say." I turned away from him and walked off.

Completely ignoring my tirade, Keyz grabbed my arm and pulled me to him. "On the real, I miss y'all. I want my family home with me," he said. He tried to hug me, but I stepped back from his embrace.

I was missing him too, but I couldn't, and wouldn't, let go of my hurt and feelings of betrayal. "You got life fucked up if you think I am going to just go on home because you claim you want your family back. What the hell did you think was going to happen when I found out about Shaun? Did you think we were going to be one big happy family?" I asked him. I jerked my arm from his grasp. "Nah, it ain't going down like that. Take your happy-go-luck ass and go play house with your other baby mama. I'm good here." I sat down on the sofa and folded my legs under me.

Keyz sat down beside me. I had hoped he would take the hint and get ghost. I pretended like I didn't notice him and stared at the TV. He started rubbing my thigh. I batted his hand away. "Go on with that bullshit," I told him. He suddenly pulled me on top of him so that I was straddling him. I felt his hardness under me. I started pounding his chest. "Let me the fuck go. Ain't nobody playing with you!" I yelled.

"Chill, bae." Ignoring my yells to stop and my punches, he started massaging my breasts. I hadn't been touched in a minute, so it was hard for me to ignore the sensation. Besides, he's the only one who had ever touched me and been inside of me, so he knew my body inside and out. He knew just where and how to touch me to get the response he wanted. One hand moved down my stomach and made its way inside my shorts. He started rubbing my clit with the tip of his fingers. I stopped resisting him altogether as my eyes closed on their own accord. A pant fell from my lips when he grounded his palm against my clit. "Let me taste it," he whispered in my ear. His words lit a fire in my core and was close to bringing me to an orgasmic state. I rocked my hips against his hand, trying to reach my climax.

I shook my head. "Aaahh," I moaned, unable to stop myself. He started rubbing faster when he elicited a moan from me. It felt so good. My pants began to come faster and faster. I bit my bottom lip when I felt the build up getting ready to explode.

"That pussy getting wet." He began to rub faster, but foolishly broke the trance and interrupted my nut when he opened his lying lips. "You coming home?" he asked me. His question was like a bucket of cold water tossed over me. My lust-filled mind cleared instantly and my eyes popped open.

Pushing him away, I squirmed out of reach. "Get the fuck away from me. You lost that privilege to touch my body." Standing up, I adjusted my shorts not able to believe I was so weak, yet again, for this nigga. *This was probably how I was so blind to all the dirt his ass did. One touch, and I let him fuck me into oblivion, I thought to myself.* He thought he could fuck me into going back home and like a weak bitch, I almost fell for it. I had to harden my heart.

"Fuck you talking about? That pussy gon' always be mine." Staring in my eyes, he put his fingers in his mouth and sucked my juices off of them. He closed his eyes and moaned a little as he savored the taste of me. My clit throbbed watching him. That shit was a serious turn on and had my juices flowing.

I rolled my eyes at him trying to down play my feelings of desire. "Whatever. It's time for you to go." I folded my arms over my chest and started tapping my foot. Anger and hurt rolled off me in waves. I was angry at myself for still wanting him and for falling for his seduction. My anger burned brighter, because he came over here and proved just how weak for him I still was.

He stood up, adjusted the erection in his jeans, and walked towards me. "Imma leave, but this conversation ain't over. I gotta go out of town for a few days. When I get back your ass coming home. Keep that pussy tight for me." He leaned down to kiss me, I turned my head away, and pushed him away from me.

"I told you it's over, Keyon. See yourself out."

"We ain't never gon' be over. The only thing that could ever end us is death," he said, causing my heart to skip a beat and shivers down my spine. Before I could respond, he left. I didn't even have a comeback for his comment, because deep in my heart I knew what he said was the truth.

Chapter 5

Be loyal to those who are not present. In doing so, you build the trust of those who are present.

-Unknown

Keyz

It's been a minute since I saw my lil' man, so when I touched down back in the N.O. after my business trip, I decided to drop by my baby mama's house and pick my son up. I sent a quick text to Ashley to let her know my plans.

Me: What's up? What my son doing?

Ashley: So you finally decide to check on your child huh?

I had to stop myself from calling and cussing her out. She knew what was up. I couldn't get mad at her tho.' I don't blame her for wanting me to take care of and spend time with my kid. Ashley might be a hoe, but she was a decent mama.

Me: Don't nobody want to hear no nagging. Just came back in town, on my way to pick up Shaun.

Ashley: I don't care what you want to hear. About time you decide to come get him.

Me: Just have him ready.

Ashley: He been ready 2 weeks ago when you missed his ball game and promised to take him to get a haircut. And you didn't bother to show up!

I felt bad that I been neglected my son. With everything that's been happening, I couldn't focus on nothing and nobody but fixing shit with my girl. I ain't had much time to do nothing else. Imma make it up and chill the whole day with him. Since my secret is out, I gotta make sure Shaun and Keira spend more time together. I knew Shaunie might be a little upset at first, but she'd come around. She wasn't gon' take nothing out on no child. I listened to *Matrimony* by Wale while I drove to pick up Shaun.

But I'm promising you better though
And your friends saying "let him go"
And we ain't getting any younger
I can give you up now,
But I can promise you forever though
It there's a question of my heart, you've got it
It don't belong to anyone but you

I listened to the lyrics of the song. The song definitely fit the situation I found myself in with Shaunie. But I ain't ever giving her up. I wouldn't know how. It was fucked up what I did, messing around with all them hoes and lying about having a kid with another woman, but I do love Shaunie with everything that's in me.

When I pulled up in front of Ashley's house, I grabbed my phone to call her so she could send Shaun outside.

"Send Shaun, I'm outside."

"Well, you got to come in and get him. I'm in the bathroom and he's asleep. The door is unlocked." She hung up the phone before I could say anything.

I got out my car, walked to her door, and went in the house. The lights were off so I flicked on the hall light and headed to Shaun's room. I stopped dead in my tracks at the sight before me when I passed by the living room. Ashley was stretched out on the floor, naked as the day she was born. Her legs were cocked open so I had a view of a dildo going in and out her wet pussy. She was so wet I saw her juices glistening from where I stood. She opened her eyes and looked at me with a smirk on her face. Picking up the pace with the dildo, she held my stare.

"Yo, what the fuck is you doing, man?" I yelled at her.

She looked down at the tent in my jeans, her smile widened. "Come and put that dick on me." She stood up and walked towards me.

"Bitch, go put on some clothes before my son walks in and sees this shit." This bitch had a whole freak show going on in the front room like she didn't have a kid living here. I had to revisit my opinion that she was a decent mother. If she pulled some shit like this to get my attention while my son was in his room asleep, God only knew what else she did when I wasn't around. I stepped back when she reached me. She tried to place her hand on my chest, but I grabbed her wrist.

"Don't act like you didn't like what you saw. I can see the evidence for myself." She jerked her hand away and tried to grab my piece.

My dick was harder than bricks. I hadn't got no pussy in almost two months, so my shit got hard for a light breeze. "That ain't for you," I growled at her, pushing her back away from me. This bitch was tripping, I ain't fucked her since she got pregnant with Shaun. *Where in the fuck this shit coming from?*

She stumbled and fell on her ass. "Fuck you, nigga. I'm tired of you telling me what I can and can't do. I can't even bring a man here to fuck me without you having shit to say." She jumped up off the floor and came in my face.

"I bought this house for my son. I didn't buy it so you can bring niggas here to get dicked down. Fuck I look like." I pushed her out my face. There was enough stuff going on in my life, I was trying not to put my hands on her and add those types of problems.

"Keep your motherfucking hands off me. I'm tired of sitting up in here being lonely, while you come and go as you please."

"What you talking about? I ain't your man and I don't live here. I can come and go whenever the fuck I want. You so fucking lonely, tell them fuck niggas to take your hoe ass to a motel or something. I don't give a fuck."

Wham! She slapped me in the face.

I tried to get my anger in check. Ashley putting her hands on me caused me to snap, I backhanded her so hard she fell to the floor. Grabbing her hair, I slapped her again and again.

"Keep your fucking hands off me." I knew I was taking a lot of my frustrations out on her, but I didn't give a fuck at this point. Seemed like every time I went inside a bitch's house, I had to beat them. Fuck, I don't even like hitting them, but these hoes didn't know how to keep their hands to themselves. I am a firm believer in equal opportunity. If a woman could hit me then bitch I was gon' beat the breaks off them. Ashley was on some other shit. We had a decent co-parenting relationship until Shaunie found out about Shaun. Before then, she knew I wasn't fucking with her on no sex level. I could never trust a bitch that trapped me with a baby by poking holes in the condom.

Standing up over her as she held her face, I glared at her. "Look, Ashley, don't put your hands on me and I will return the favor. Now, where the fuck is my son?"

"Get the fuck out! My son ain't going a fucking step," she yelled.

Ignoring her outburst, I shook my head in disgust at her sorry ass, went to Shaun's room, lifted my sleeping son in my arms and carried him out the house. I had to get out of there before I really hurt Ashley. As I placed Shaun in the back seat of the car, Ashley came running outside in a robe. She was screaming obscenities at me about taking her son. I locked the door when she tried to open it to remove Shaun.

"Open the door, Keyz. I want my son." She began banging on the window, waking Shaun up and he started to cry at the commotion his mama caused.

"Back the fuck up, Ashley. I ain't playing with your simple ass."

"You ain't about to take my son and go play no fucking house. That hoe better go play house with that dead baby." She backed away with bulging eyes when she realized what she said. She looked to the left and then to the right as if seeking help.

I saw red. Baby mama or not, this bitch was dead. Before I could think, I opened the door and grabbed my gun.

"Dad, I'm scared," Shaun cried, bringing me out of my homicidal haze. On the strength on my son, I put my gun back under the seat and turned to stare at the bitch that tried to ruin my life with her conniving ways. She stood before me trembling with her mouth opening and closing as she searched for words to say. There was no words to say to fix what she said. I looked at her with cold eyes filled with murder and hoped my look conveyed my thoughts. She was dead to me.

Chapter 6

*Be sure to put your love and loyalty in the right place and stand
firm in that love and loyalty.*

-Tess Calomino

Shaunie

The elevator doors opened with a soft whoosh. I stepped out and
walked into the outer office of King's Realty, located downtown in
the CBD. I decided to move forward with my separation from
Keyz.

My conversation with my mom really helped me to put things
into perceptive. The first step was getting my own place. I knew I
could stay with my mom indefinitely if I chose, but I enjoyed
having my own. My next step was following my dream of opening
a daycare center, so I was going to began looking for a building. I
walked to the reception area where a middle-aged lady sat behind a
mahogany desk.

"Good afternoon. May I help you?" the receptionist asked with
a warm, inviting smile.

Feeling and looking more like my old self, I smiled back. When I woke up, I actually felt good. I decided to get my hair and nails done before my appointment. My body was wrapped in a simple BeBe maxi dress with strappy flat Chanel scandals on my feet.

"Good afternoon. My name is Shaunie Williams. I have a one o'clock appointment with Mr. Dametrius King." When I told my mom about my plans to search for a house, she tried to convince me to stay with her. However, I was adamant that I wanted to move, so she asked around for a good realty company with great agents. King's Realty came highly recommended. I was leery of using the agent who Keyz and I usually work with, because I wasn't sure he hadn't fucked her, too.

"I'll let Mr. King know you are here. Please have a seat."

I took a seat in one of the plush chairs, watching as she picked up the receiver and briefly spoke into it. "He will be with you shortly. Would you like any refreshments while you wait?" she asked me.

"No, thank you. I'm fine." I looked around the office. There were several paintings of historical sites located in the city, painted by some of New Orleans finest and greatest local artists. The rest were paintings and portraits by world renowned artists. One painting in particular caught my eye and enraptured me. It was a painting that depicted a couple embracing and sharing a passionate kiss. The couple is oblivious to everything around them. They were so in tuned to each other that their faces are indistinguishable. Viewers couldn't tell where the man began or where the women ended.

I was so into the painting that I didn't hear anyone walking up to me. "That's one of my favorite paintings. It's titled *The Kiss*..."

"...by Edvard Munch," I stated before he could complete his thought. I turned around and looked at the owner of the voice. He seemed familiar, but I couldn't place him. Mr. King was a very attractive man who stood about six feet tall and looked very distinguished dressed in a tailor made gray suit, crisp white shirt, and a blue tie.

"Intelligent and beautiful. I love a woman who knows her art." He extended his hand for me to shake. "I'm Dametrius King. It's a pleasure to meet you, Ms. Williams."

"Likewise," I said, standing up. I shook his hand. He held my hands a moment longer than what would be deemed professional. I quickly placed my hand behind my back, because the pleasant sensation of the brief contact confused me.

He stared at me as if he knew he had an effect on me. It wasn't a cocky stare, just a knowing one. "Let's go in my office. I walked behind him until we reached a door that I assumed was his office. "Ladies first," he said as he motioned with his hand for me to precede him into the room. He closed the door and walked around to his desk. "Please have a seat." He remained standing until I sat down.

His office was nicely appointed with opulent furnishings. Behind his desk was a floor to ceiling window that overlooked the river. The view was breathtaking.

"Thank you. I appreciate you taking this appointment on such short notice."

"It's no problem at all. So, what can I help you with today?" he asked me. He stared at me with his eyes unblinking. It felt like he was studying me.

"I am interested in purchasing a home asap. As I stated when I spoke to you yesterday, I have a list of features that I'm interested in. These features are nonnegotiable. " I said, getting right down to business.

Chuckling, he said, "I see you already have an idea of what you want. I can take your preferences and search for any listings that match." He took notes as I told him what I was looking for. "I have several homes listed that match your criteria. Let's set an appointment to view a few of them. What dates and times are you available?"

"I'm pretty much available all week. The sooner the better."

"I have an opening on Friday at two. I can line up some properties for your viewing."

"That's perfect. I can't wait," I said excitedly.

His eyes dropped to my cleavage and he subtly licked his lips. I fidgeted in my chair a bit. "I'm sorry for staring. I just realized that I met you before, a while back, at a nightclub. I asked if I could buy you a drink and you turned me down. I'm Dam."

That's why he seemed familiar. "Yes, I remember you now. I'm sorry, I'm not good at remembering names and faces." I lied through my teeth, dropping my head for a second. While I may not have remembered his name, I definitely remembered his face, especially his dimples. He had the deepest set of dimples that I had ever seen. He was light skinned with light brown eyes and a chiseled jawline. His black wavy hair was cut in low fade. Seeing this handsome man subtly flirt with me made me realized all that I missed out on being with Keyz. I never had the chance to play the field and see the different options.

"So, is there a Mr. Williams that will be joining us as we look at the properties?" He glanced at my ring finger before he tapped his pen on the desk.

"No, just me," I said, keeping it short. No need to elaborate that Keyz and I split. I grabbed my purse and stood up to leave.

He followed suit. "It's been a pleasure. Please let me know if you have any questions."

We walked out of his office. I thought he would leave me at the door of his office, but he walked me to the reception area. I continued to walk towards the bank of elevators. I felt him staring a hole in my back. *Walk normal and don't look back*, I chanted in my head. I stepped on the elevator when it whooshed opened. I made eye contact with Dametrius. He was leaning against the reception counter, giving me a smoldering look. When the elevators started closing, he winked at me. I was momentarily stunned by his open display of flirtation. I gave him a soft smile as the elevator closed. *What the hell, I'm single and ready to mingle!*

Chapter 7

Bad faith likes discourse on friendship and loyalty.

-Mason Cooley

Keyz

I pulled up at a dilapidated house that served as a meeting spot for me and my inner circle. One would never suspect the house occasionally had occupants. It was a dingy white shotgun house, filthy with grime located in the poverty stricken area in the lower ninth ward. The neighborhood was basically abandoned. Aluminum foil covered the windows and bars prevented unsolicited entry. The building should have been condemned long ago by the city, but as long as they got the property tax payments, the inspector's office didn't complain. It was a muggy night and the humidity didn't help the old musty smell that permeated from the old dwelling. Checking my surroundings, I got out the car with my gun in my hand.

I bounded up the steps and used my key to open the door. Short of patience, I entered the house. When I entered the kitchen, I nodded at the dawgs. My eyebrows were drawn together to indicate my confusion at the absence of Qwan and Killer. Usually the whole inner circle met up for emergency meetings. I took a seat and drummed my fingers on the table. Rayne called an emergency meeting at two in the morning, so I knew something was up.

"What's up, Rayne?" I asked, anxious to find out why. I knew it was important, because Rayne was a man of few words. When he spoke, anyone with two ears better listen.

Rayne leaned forward as he spoke. "You know the shipment that Alejandor sent out yesterday was due to come in tonight?" We nodded our heads to confirm. "Someone set up a hit on it." He leaned back waiting on our reactions. It was his job to make sure all the incoming shipments where handled. He was the first line of communication for the delivery drivers.

I exploded out of my chair so fast, the chair flew back and slammed into the wall. I huffed as rage washed through me like a hurricane. My temper had always been bad, but lately with all the shit I had been going through, it had been explosive. Usually, I would think before I responded, because not controlling my temper in this business could be dangerous and get a nigga killed. A boss couldn't be ruled by his emotions.

"The fucking street value of the product is over three and half million dollars!" The shipment contained 21 keys of pure uncut cocaine. I picked up the nearest thing I could find and flung it into the wall, ready to smash someone's brain in. I began to pace back and forth. Stopping in the middle of the floor, I pinched the bridge of my nose in an effort to calm myself down. "What fucking time and where at?" The only motherfuckers who knew about the shipment was my people and Alejandro's. I counted Alejandro out, because a nigga that has a net worth over a billion dollars wasn't gon' risk it for what he considered pocket change. But that didn't mean his goons wouldn't.

"Shit just ain't been right around here lately. We been having too many fucking slip ups," Thugga said, banging his fist on the table.

"Before y'all get too amped up, hear me out," said Rayne. He placed his elbows on the table and interlocked his fingers.

I looked at this nigga like he was crazy. How the fuck is he that calm when he just informed someone that they lost out on that type of money and product? Trying to keep a clear head, I sat down so I could listen to what he had to say.

"It's been some funny shit lately with the traps getting hit. You and Thugga been busying with y'all's problems, so I made a decision for the team. I had been getting bad vibes about shit, so I followed my gut and planned differently for this shipment. I changed the routes and vehicles for all but one of our usual carriers. The driver was shot execution style and left on the side of the interstate near the drop off spot. The driver only had three keys in the vehicle. That's all that was snatched," Rayne said. "But the dumb fucker who jacked the driver dropped his fucking phone." He pulled out a Ziploc bag with a phone in it.

I was happy that he had the phone that could give me a lead, but I was also pressed about my product. "So where is the rest of the product?" I asked him. I could feel my blood pressure starting to boil.

"I put it in a storage locker on the Westbank. I didn't bring it to the usual spot, because that would defeat the purpose of why I planned it the way I planned it."

Some of the tension drained from my body at the news that most of my product wasn't gone. The loss of the profit from the product would have been a big hit. Not enough to put me down for the count, but a loss nevertheless. Nobody was gon' take a hit like that laying down. Plus, I wasn't trying to help another nigga build an empire from my hard work. Rayne was on point with his business. I gave him a head nod to let him know I appreciated him staying on top of the game.

"Man, what the fuck is you saying?" Thugga asked Rayne.

Choosing his words wisely, he answered, "The only people who knew about the shipment was Alejandro's people and our people. If Alejandro's people was behind this, they would have followed all the vehicles taking different routes. However, the only vehicle that was hit was the one we mapped out together as a crew. Whoever hit the shipment or informed someone of the shipment knew our plan and our route." Rayne looked at us. "Someone from our team is working and plotting against us and not like the little beef we had with Boobie. I'm thinking that bullshit with Qwan was a distraction from this hit here."

"So where in the fuck is Qwan and Killer?" I asked.

I was lost in thought thinking about who could be fucking with my business. I thought we handled everyone that was associated with Boobie. Maybe we underestimated his connection to everything.

"I didn't call them. The only niggas I trust is sitting at this table." He got quiet and let us digest that fact.

"You sure the place wasn't tapped?" Thugga asked Rayne.

"Man, I swept the place myself when we met."

It was hard for me to think that Qwan or Killer would betray our team. Yeah, I was the boss, but I made sure my niggas was eating good, too. I made executive decisions because at the end of the day, I made this, but I always got their take on matters. Putting my head down for a second, I came up with a quick plan to ferry out the culprit. "In our team meetings, we will continue to map out routes and plans together so we don't let whoever know we are on to them."

At their head nods, I continued. "Rayne, you continue to map out different routes, but make sure you run it by me." I pointed to my chest while staring intently at him. I appreciated he looked out for me and the team, but I felt a lil' salty that he didn't run it by me.

"I'm on it, boss," he replied, without any shade or feelings, just business.

To soften my reminder to him I was the boss, I nodded in his direction. "Good looking out, my nigga." He returned the nod. "I want phone records for Killer and Qwan and surveillance on them from the traps they visit. If they are playing for both teams, they had to have left a trail somewhere." The plan was to check their phone calls to see if any numbers matched to the number from the phone that was left at the scene. I was a ruthless boss, but tried my best to be fair. My first instinct was to kill first, ask questions later, then examine info. But that could be dangerous for a boss. In all my business dealings, I thought everything out. Scenarios played in my mind until I chose the best outcome.

"If they are?" Rayne asked.

"Then they could get it like any other nigga," I said, not missing a beat.

"Man, that's some fuck up shit, if they are betraying the team. We worked too hard to get to the top for one of our own to bring us down." Thugga stood up and starting pacing back and forth.

After losing Taz, I didn't want to lose another one of my dawgs. The five of us had been tight since E.H. Phillips Jr. High school. We were all lil' bad ass motherfuckers terrorizing the neighborhood growing up, but if one of them was betraying me, I wasn't gon' have a problem putting his lights out.

Chapter 8

There are many who love in this world, but few who are loyal.

-Arabic Proverb

Shaunie

Standing in front of the floor length mirror, I admired myself. I was unquestionably feeling myself, because I was on fleek from head to toe. My hair was bone straight to the middle of my back and eyebrows were freshly waxed. A rose pink Cavalli wrap dress, that complimented my skin tone, encased my luscious petite frame and I rocked a pair of Giuseppe nude stiletto heels. The vibration from my cell phone stopped me from continuing to check myself out. I grabbed my phone from the vanity and saw I had a message from Nikki. I opened the message and read it. *Hurry bitch. We outside.*

I grabbed my gold clutch, walked down the stairs, and went into the living room to tell my mom I was leaving.

"I am about to leave, mom," I said as I bent down towards a sleeping Keira. Brushing her silky curls out of her face, I kissed her cheek.

My mom smiled up at me. "You look really nice, honey. I'm so glad you are finally getting out the house and going to enjoy yourself."

"Thanks, mom. It feels good to get dressed up. I won't be out too long."

"Baby, go and enjoy your night. You are still young," she said with a meaningful look.

My mom thought I was too young to settle down with Keyz at eighteen. I didn't respond to her comment. Sometimes the heart wants what it wants. Even though times were different back then, my mom wasn't much older than I was when she met and married my dad.

I walked out the door and hopped in the car with my girls. The scent of weed permeated the smoked filled car. I knew they lit one up on the way to get me.

"Hey, my besties. I'm so ready to turn up," I said when I got in the car.

Stacy pushed the blunt to me from the front seat. I wasn't a big smoker, but I'd hit a blunt every now and then. "Girl, you trying to get fucked up with that tight ass dress on. Keyz would flip the fuck out if he knew you had that shit on," Stacy said.

I wasn't worried about Keyz. He told me he was going out of town, so that wouldn't be an issue. Anyway, we weren't together anymore. I hit the blunt and blew the smoke out before I responded back to her.

"Fuck a Keyz. He is not my concern and I'm damn sure not his. He can do him like he has been doing all these years behind my back and I will do me." I wasn't looking to do me. Getting out of the house and having a little fun was all I was after. Passing the blunt back up front, Nikki took it.

"Girl, motherfuck Keyz. She ain't got to answer to him about shit. He ain't her fucking daddy. He did *her* wrong. Not the other way around," Nikki said hitting the weed. She was still upset about everything that went down. I swear she was taking Keyz' betrayal worse than I was. She was so loyal to me and such a ride or die friend. I tried to shelter her from my pain as much as I could, because Nikki could go from zero to one hundred in the blink of an eye. I didn't want her and Keyz to have any words that would lead to beef. That situation would be disastrous. Nikki is my best friend and the girl friend of Keyz' best friend, Thugga. If Nikki and Keyz beef, then Thugga and I would be in the middle.

Nikki, Stacy, and I went to the grand opening of a club located downtown. The place was jammed packed. Wiz Khalifa and Iggy's

Go Hard or Go Home blasted through the speakers in the club. We made our way to the bar before we hit the floor. A nice looking tall dude with dreads and gold teeth offered to buy our drinks and we let him. Usually I didn't accept drink offers from men out of respect for Keyz, but what the fuck. He can get pussy, the least I could do is get a drink. I winked at the dude who got our drinks.

With our drinks in our hands, we moved to the dance floor and started dancing. I started twerking to the beat. Some random dude came behind me and I continued to dance on him. I felt his dick swelling in his pants and I wanted to laugh. Ain't shit popping.

"What the fuck they doing here?" Stacy said. I looked around to see what she was talking about.

"Who are you talking about?" I asked her as I turned away from the dude. The weed and alcohol had me in my zone.

She had a glare on her face as she pointed to the right of us. Close by the DJ booth stood Keyz, Killer, Thugga, Rayne, and a few of the goons from their clique. I was slightly annoyed, because Keyz told me he was going out of town for a few days and I didn't feel like dealing with him tonight. There was no way he would pass up the opportunity to try and convince me to take his ass back.

"Killer told me they had business to take care of out the city. I so did not want to run into them clowns tonight," Stacy said, sipping her drink.

Nikki smacked her teeth and rolled her eyes when she spotted Thugga. "Fuck it. Imma act like I don't see Thugga's ass and I hope y'all ignore y'all niggas, too. I'm trying to turn up and don't need them fucking it up," Nikki said. She turned back around and started dancing. I shrugged my shoulder and continued to dance.

I was grinding my hips to a song when I felt hands slide around my waist and someone's breath near my ear. I started to move away until I heard Keyz' voice whisper in my ear.

"What you got on, ma? You trying to get fucked up wearing this tight ass shit. You got all my pussy and ass on display for another nigga to see." I smelled the alcohol on his breath.

Between the weed and the alcohol, Keyz' voice had me in a trance. His breath against my ear caused my panties to be soaked and my clit to throb. "I can wear whatever the hell I want. And it's my pussy and ass to show." My words came out in a pant. Wanting to tease him, I grinded harder on his now hard dick that I felt poking my back. I wasn't drunk or high enough where I was going to go home with him and fuck him. My hateful feelings made me tease him until he begged me and still I wasn't going to give in.

"You coming home today, Shaunie? A nigga missing you and that wet pussy. I want to suck that pussy from the back."

His words were seducing me. I wanted to be with him tonight. My body was craving him. However, my mind and feelings refused to submit. I stepped back and looked at him.

"I thought you told me the other day you were going out of town?" I questioned him. I didn't trust shit he said anymore. Whenever his lips moved, I knew a lie was going to sprout out.

"I did go out of town and now I'm back." Keyz tried to pull me closer to him, but I wanted answers.

"Well, I didn't hear from you. Why didn't you let me know you were back so you could come and get Keira? Or were you with a hoe?" I asked with fifty shades of doubt in my voice. The corner of my upper lip curved slightly in a sneer. I folded my hands across my chest and tilted my head to the side.

He huffed out a breath and narrowed his eyes at me. "I done told you plenty of times I ain't fucking with nobody. I'm getting tired of this going back and forth shit. What's it gon' be, huh? You coming with me tonight or what?" Keyz asked me.

I wanted to go, but I didn't want to look stupid by falling back with him so soon. Even if my mind didn't agree, my heart knew if I went over to the house with Keyz, there was a huge chance I wasn't leaving. Me giving in to him so soon and without consequences would just allow him to fall back to his old ways with his fucked up behavior. If and when I decided we would get back together, he had to earn my body, heart, and trust. I shook my head no.

He stepped back from me and nodded his head. Watching as he turned and went to the bar, I saw a tall chick with a model type body walk up to him and start a conversation. Not knowing what was being said pissed me off. Keyz was cheesed up in this hoe's face like he didn't have a care in the world. I didn't know if he was doing that to make me mad or not, but he shouldn't have been smiling. He shouldn't get to enjoy life when I was drowning in misery. Even though I just rejected his advances, it hurt to see him talking to someone else.

Nikki and Stacy pulled me back in the crowd to dance. I wanted to go home after dealing with Keyz and seeing him entertain some chick, but I allowed my friends to cheer me up. We began to twerk to a hot bounce beat. I felt someone come up behind me. I didn't bother turning around, because I thought it was Keyz coming to convince me to go with him again. I kept dancing and twerking to the beat against his body.

Abruptly, I was snatched from behind and spun around to face Keyz. I scrunched up my face in confusion for a second until I looked down and saw a dude on the ground in the club. I looked up into Keyz' face and knew he was pissed. My mouth started opening and closing as I tried to find the words to explain what happened. My heart rate accelerated at the look of fury in his eyes. He gripped my forearm and started to drag me from the club. I heard Nikki and Stacy screaming at him to let me go.

When we got outside, he pushed me up against the wall and got in my face. He clenched his fist, placed them on the wall beside my head, and leaned closer to me. "What the fuck is you thinking acting like that in public? You trying to get that nigga killed up in there?"

"First off, I thought that was you behind me. Secondly, you can cheese up in a hoe's face, but I can't dance with someone else? You have lost your rabbit ass mind," I said. I pushed his chest to get him away from me. Our confrontation had attracted bystanders who were waiting to see what would happen.

"You belong to me. Ain't another nigga about to step up on what's mine. Take your ass home and get out of that slutty ass dress," he said, grabbing my arm. Wide–eyed and mouth opened, I gasped in shock at the way he spoke to me. He had never spoken so harsh to me before. I jerked away and slapped him across the face. He grabbed my hand to stop the other incoming slap. I couldn't believe he would stand there and talk to me as if I was another hoe he was fucking with. His aggression and attitude towards me would make one think I was the one fucking around and tearing our family apart.

"You think you can do whatever the fuck you want. I put up with you and those bitches. You fucked around on me countless times. Your hoe from the video even had the audacity to taunt me about y'alls sex tape, but you up in my face about a dance, Keyz. Really?" Here he was practically throwing a tantrum over a dance. At the same time he was pressuring me to come home, he was laughing and joking with bitches at the bar.

"Wait, when the fuck you seen that bitch?"

"That night I went out with Stacy. She approached me talking shit." I saw recognition in his eyes as I refreshed his memory. We never had a chance to really address the fight I had with the chick he was fucking with because we got distracted talking about the actual sex tape and not the hoe that starred in it. Keyz made a grab for me, but I stepped away. I was tired of him and his shit. "You think you can fuck around on me and I'm supposed to be okay with that. Hell no! You got me all the way fucked up. So fucking what if I wanted to dance with another nigga. Newsflash, we are not together. I could fuck another nigga if I wanted to!" I yelled in his face.

Wham! Keyz slapped me in my face. I stumbled on my heels, but remained upright. I grabbed my cheek and look at him with tears of anger. "Don't ever say no shit like that!" he said. He grabbed my arms and shook me until my teeth rattled. I heard my friends screaming for someone to let them go. I assumed they were being held by Killer and Thugga to stop them from interfering.

When he let me go, I rushed on him swinging. I got a good lick to his lip, because it split open and started bleeding. I wasn't taking no hits without fighting back. "Fuck you! I hate you!" I pulled back and looked him dead in the eyes. "For every bitch you fucked while you were with me, Imma fuck two niggas!" I instantly regretted it when I said it, because I knew I went too far. The vein in his forehead throbbed and he clenched his teeth. He wrapped his hands around my slender neck and squeezed.

"Let me fucking go, Thugga. He's hurting her. You know she ain't mean that shit. Nigga, let me go," Nikki said. She elbowed Thugga in the side, causing him to grunt.

Rayne walked up to Keyz and tried to pry his hands from me. "Keyz, let her go man before y'all do more than what y'all regret right now."

"Killer, get that nigga. He done gon' too fucking far. Get him. She can't fucking breathe!" Stacy screamed. She tried to wrestle her way from Killer's grasp to no avail.

I raked my nails up and down Keyz' arms. He didn't even appear to feel it. Never seeing this side of him, I was scared. I was struggling to breathe as my feet dangled off the ground. I used my feet to kick him, but he didn't seem to feel it. My heel landed to his groin, but either he was too far gone to feel it or I didn't kick hard enough. "Keyon," I rasped out. Me calling his name seemed to snap him out of his anger. He loosened his hold on my neck and stepped away from me. I slid down the wall, wheezing from a lack of air.

The fury from Keyz' face drained away. He stood wide-eyed in shock. Shocked at his actions or shocked at my words, I knew not. Nikki and Stacy ran to me and helped me to stand up. "Bae, I'm sorry, I didn't mean for that to happen," Keyz said. He walked closer to me. I wanted to fight back, but I was so shocked that he would choke me like that. For the first time since we had been together, I saw the Keyz that everyone saw on the streets. The dangerous part of him that he kept lurking, but masked when he was around me. I was chilled to the bone with fear. A small tremble racked my body.

"Back the fuck away from her motherfucker! I swear if I had a gun I would splatter your brains on the fucking wall," Nikki screamed, getting in Keyz' face.

Thugga grabbed Nikki's arm. "Chill with that. Don't be disrespecting that man. That's between him and Shaunie."

They began to argue. Keyz walked up to me with his eyes full of remorse. He hugged me. I tried to move away from him, but he didn't let me go. He used his fingers to tilt my face towards him, forcing me to look at him. "I was wrong. Don't ever say no shit like that. Don't disrespect yourself trying to get even for the shit I did."

Seeing the look of sincerity in his eyes, I nodded my head. "This was the last straw, Keyon. You shouldn't ever put your hands on me." I wasn't down for no type of relationship where the man and woman fight, but stayed together. Those games weren't for me.

He leaned closer so only I could hear what he said. "I know and I'm sorry. Let's go home and talk about it. Just give me a chance." His eyes pleaded.

"Why should I? You 'round here cheating and making babies like you ain't in a relationship. Now, you putting your hands on me. Since when do men do all that to the women they claim to love? I can't even dance with someone without you acting a plum fucking fool, but it's okay for you to do all the shit you do and I'm supposed to just accept you back because you asked?"

Keyz had really lost his damn mind, thinking I would want to talk after he had just choked me outside of the club. Eventually, we would talk, but it wasn't anytime soon. My hurt and pain would make me do and say things I didn't want to. I wanted to pick up the nearest thing and use it as a weapon against him. The devil on my left shoulder tried to convince me to hurt him physically as bad as he hurt me emotionally, but I restrained myself because I knew jail wouldn't be a pretty look for me. Dealing with him had me acting so out of character with all this fussing and cussing. At this point, I didn't know how to act around him, except with bitterness. I didn't like the person I was becoming. I was never the type of person to harbor negative feelings. So for the time being and until I could resist my evil thoughts, we needed time apart.

I shook my head at him. He just didn't get it. "There are no more chances." I jerked away from him and backed away. Keyz looked like he wanted to follow me, but didn't. I turned around and noticed a lot of bitches smirking as I passed by. I guessed they enjoyed the show of Keyz knocking me from the pedestal he placed me on. Holding my head high, refusing to let them see the humiliation I was feeling, I walked passed the crowd to Nikki's car with Nikki and Stacy following behind me. Keyz stared at me through the window. I turned my head away from him, but I could still feel his eyes burning a hole through me.

Nikki got in the driver's seat. "Are you okay, Shaunie?" She caught my eyes in the rear view mirror. Nikki of all people knew what I was going through. Not only had she dealt with Thugga repeatedly stepping out on her, but she'd been on the receiving end of his abuse, too. The sympathy in her eyes told me how much this shit hurt her. I think she was more disappointed in Keyz than I was, because he was the hope she held on to for a better life. Her hope probably came tumbling down the moment he laid his hands on me.

The tears that I held back threatened to choke me, but I refused to shed another tear behind him. I nodded my head. My throat was on fire and I couldn't verbally respond. I knew I shouldn't have said that to Keyz. He was not the kind of man to take kindly to threats. Tonight, we both said and did things we regretted. I knew we would never be the same again.

Chapter 9

Loyalty means I am down with you whether you are wrong or right, but I will tell you when you are wrong and help you get it right.

-Unknown

Keyz

It was a warm day in May, so I decided to go check on my car wash business. Warmer weather always had the car wash swamped. I sat behind my desk, put my head in my hands and thought back to two days ago when me and Shaunie had the fight outside the club. Letting my bad temper get the best of good reasoning, my anger spiraled out of control when I put my hands on Shaunie. My mama had been warning me my entire life to watch my temper, less I do something I'd later regret. Waves of regret relentlessly washed over me, and I felt awful for treating my girl like that. My anger was ridiculous and misplaced over her dancing with another dude and the crazy shit she said in the heat of the moment. At the mention of her giving my pussy to another nigga, I saw red. That shit had me going in a rage. I knew I was wrong for hitting and choking my girl. Still, I would dead any nigga for laying hands on my daughter, her reckless talk or not.

Once I had time to cool off and think about the conversation we had before I spazzed out on her ass, I remembered she mentioned NeNe approached her in the club and threw the sex tape shit in her face before they starting fighting. I forgot about getting at NeNe stupid ass because of everything that had been going on, but I was gone rectify that shit today.

There was three loud knocks at the door before someone pushed it open. Rayne came through the door.

"Yo, my nigga, what's good?" I asked him.

"Man, I dipped through to get my mom's car washed. Sammie told me you were back here. What up with you?" Rayne took a seat in the chair that was in front of my desk.

"Chilling. Trying get caught up on business."

"On some real shit, about the other night with you and Shaunie, that was fucked up, my nigga."

I wasn't offended that Rayne called me out on that bullshit. He was the type of nigga that was gon' tell someone when they were wrong and help them to make it right. Plus, he had four sisters, so he was sensitive when it came to innocent women being beat by men. That didn't mean he wouldn't murk a bitch that was up to no good.

"I already know. That shit just got all out of proportion. It was the first and last time I would ever put my hands on her. My temper got the best of me. I don't know why I even reacted that way, because I knew she said that shit out of anger." Remorse hung over me like a black cloud, I felt a tightening in my chest and a lump form in my throat.

Shaunie wasn't the type of chick to be 'round here fucking and sucking different niggas 'cause the mood struck. A nigga was gon' have to work for her pussy.

"I thought I was going to have to shoot at your ass to get you off her. Your ass straight zoned out." He laughed. "I wasn't gon' let you go too far and hurt her. Them other niggas acted like they were scared to interfere."

They probably were. It was hard for me to step back from the ledge once my anger exploded to a certain point. I almost killed Ashley stupid ass the other day for her comment, until my son cried. The only thing that could keep me sane was Shaunie and my kids.

"Good looking out. You know I didn't mean to go too far with my girl. I appreciate you stepping in." After that, I realized I need to give both of us some space to get over the other night. It might be wise to give Shaunie some time to figure herself out, but I was afraid if I gave her too much time she wouldn't come back to me. *Why should she?* I thought. After everything I did to her, I really don't deserve her. She had no reason to come back to me, because all she had to go off of was my word to do right. But I hadn't given her a reason to believe my words. My actions proved to her that my words weren't shit. She was everything a man could want and more, but I messed over her and fucked it all up. I needed to prove myself to her, but I didn't know where to start.

Leaning back in the leather chair in my office, I puffed some loud, and let the flow of pleasure hum through me. I needed something to calm me as I contemplated on how to get rid of NeNe after I found out about the tape. Not knowing the hows and whys behind the sex tape and pictures was fucking with me.

"I need to get at NeNe. A few months back, I stopped fucking with her and she threatened to tell Shaunie about me and her. I didn't think nothing of it. Then someone sent pictures and a tape to the house for Shaunie to see."

A muscle tickled in his jaw. "That's why I don't fuck with these hoes. They be on some bullshit." I knew he was thinking of Michelle and Tiffany. Five years ago, Rayne was in a relationship with Michelle, a girl he had known since they were twelve years ago. At the same time, he was fucking with Tiffany on the side. Rayne refused to leave Michelle for Tiffany. She starting getting too attached and demanding more than what side hoes get, so he broke it off. What he didn't know was that Tiffany was bipolar and didn't take too well when denied things she wanted. She broke into Rayne's and Michelle's house one night while he was out and killed Michelle then herself. Before she killed herself, she left a note saying since she couldn't have what she wanted, then neither could he. Rayne found them both in the house the next morning. He hadn't been the same since then.

Even after Rayne's love triangle ended tragically, I still fucked around. When a person is removed from a situation, they don't think shit like that would happen to them. Now, I knew that it could. If NeNe was bold enough to get with someone to sabotage my life by sending pictures and a video, then no telling what extremes she was willing to go to.

"Fa real, Fa real," I said as I rubbed my hands down my face.

"What you need me to do?"

I had planned to go to her house and beat her ass, but seeing how the last time ended, I wasn't putting myself in that situation again. Moreover, I didn't trust myself not to kill her on the spot before I got the info I needed.

"Pick her ass up, and take her to the warehouse. Don't fuck her up too much. I need info on how she got those pictures and how she knew where I lived to send them."

Rayne nodded his head. "I ain't gon' overdo it, but Imma show the snake bitch I mean business."

He could do whatever he wanted to the bitch as long as she was able to talk when I reached her. Knowing that hoe, she probably was gon' sing like a bird and rat on everybody. Loose lips sink ships and she had proven she couldn't keep hers shut. If she didn't talk, I was going to relish torturing the info out of her. The first body part I was going to started on was her wagging ass tongue. I was gon' cut it out and send it to her mama as a gift from her soon to be dearly departed daughter. The bitch wouldn't be able to talk, but the hoe would still have her fingers to write, before I cut those off, too.

Chapter 10

I really don't expect or ask much from people. Just loyalty and honesty.

-Unknown

Shaunie

My high heels clacked on the polished hardwood floor as I followed Dametrius around the home he showed me.

"As you can see, all of the specifications you requested comes standard in the custom built home. What do you think?"

The house was perfect for me and Keira. It was a two-story house with four bedrooms and three bathrooms. On the ground floor was the kitchen, living room, dining room, and the guest room. There was a terrace and a swimming pool included.

"I love it. This is the one," I said with excitement. I was looking forward to moving into my new place. This would be my first time living alone. After the debacle the other day with Keyz outside of the club, I was ready to put all the drama behind me and move forward with my life.

"Great. I will put in the offer today."

"Tell the seller I want to pay in cash and by the end of the week." I had my own money, thanks to the trust fund my dad set up for me, but courtesy of Keyz' personal account where I was an authorized person to withdraw funds, I was getting a new house with new top of the line furniture. Hell, I may even get a new car. Dametrius looked at me with a surprised expression on his face and his eyebrows slanted upwards. "Will that be a problem?" I raised my eyebrows.

He chuckled. "Not at all, Ms. Williams. I'll have the paperwork in two days. I'll make arrangements with the title company and get back with you about the day, time and location to close."

The shrill ringing of my cell phone interrupted us. I looked at the screen and almost rolled my eyes. *What does he want?*

"Excuse me. I have to take this call." Pushing the accept button, I walked into another room for privacy.

"Yes, Keyon." I said his name like it was distasteful on my tongue.

He sighed into the phone. "I told you I was sorry about the other day, bae. Please kill the attitude." I wanted him to respect my wishes for space and leave me the hell alone, but he didn't seem to get it.

Barely containing the retort from leaving my mouth, I compressed my lips. He acted as if sorry made all his fuck-ups better. "What do you need? I don't have Keira with me and I'm sort of busy right now."

"I wanted to come and pick up Keira this weekend." That would work out good for me. I would be able to move without worrying about her getting in the way.

"Yeah. That's fine. I will most likely be moving in my place this weekend anyway and I could use that time to get things settled."

"Shaunie, you know you don't have to do that. I'll leave the house for y'all if you really don't want me there."

I knew he would, but that house had too many bad memories for me. A new start is what I wanted and needed. "I'm cool. I don't want to live there."

"You want me and the crew to help you move?"

It would be so much easier to let him come to the rescue and do it for me, but I had to learn to stand on my own two feet. "Thanks, but no. I don't need you rescuing me. I think I can handle arranging a moving company."

He didn't say anything for a few seconds. "Alright. Just send me the address so I can have the security company come and set up." I was reluctant to accept his offer, because I really didn't want Keyz to have no part of my life that didn't involve Keira, but I understood his concerns. "Please, bae. Y'all my family. I ain't gon' rest until I know y'all are protected," he said when I didn't respond.

"Okay. I'll text you the address. That doesn't mean you can just pop up whenever you want either. I'm serious about us being done."

"What I tell you? We ain't ever gon' be done. Imma respect your decision and give you some space, but we still together."

I rolled my eyes to the heavens. This fool just didn't want to get it. I was done. Point blank period. "Whatever. I gotta go."

"Wait," Keyz said when I was about to hang up.

"What now?"

"Imma have Shaun with me, too." Keyz dropped that bomb.

My feelings were mixed. I didn't want my daughter to not be around her brother because I was having a hard time accepting the situation. Anyway, she had obviously been around him before. "Okay," I said in a small voice. Keyz bringing up Shaun solidified my decision to move on. My reaction to the kid's name assured me that I was doing the right thing. I didn't want Keyz to be forced to choose between me and his son, because I didn't think I would ever be okay about it.

"I'm sorry, bae. I destroyed our relationship. I love you."

"There's nothing to be sorry for, because it wouldn't change a fucking thing. It's over and done. I don't have a problem with Keira being around Shaun, but do not bring her anywhere around his ghetto ass ma. I mean that shit. I will take you to court for custody and everything you have, if I hear one fucking thing about it." I knew Keyz wouldn't let anyone hurt Keira, but I didn't trust no bitch with my child. These hoes could be vindictive.

"Shaunie, you know me better than that."

"If I knew you better than I fucking thought, we wouldn't be having this conversation, now would we?" I said yelling into the phone. I was starting to get pissed.

"I hear ya. I'll be by on Friday." He hung up.

Shaking my head as I put my phone back into my purse, I turned around and Dametrius was leaning against the doorway. I jumped and placed my hand over my pounding heart. "You scared the crap out of me."

"Sorry, I didn't mean to scare you."

"What are you doing standing behind me all silent like a serial killer, listening in on people's conversation?"

He stared at me like a lion would a lamb. The hunger in his eyes was hard to ignore, but I did. I was more worried about why he stood behind me while I had a conversation on the phone.

"I came to check on you when you started yelling on your phone call. Is everything okay? You sounded pretty pissed."

"I'm just peachy and I stepped out for privacy, so you coming to check on me was unwarranted," I snapped at him.

He put his hands up like he was surrendering. "I apologize and I wasn't trying to eavesdrop. I was just worried, because you were obviously upset."

Ignoring his apology, I walked next to him as we went out the door. The sun was blazing down on us and the heat was sure to smear the makeup on my neck that I put on to hide my bruises. I couldn't bear seeing the reminder of Keyz putting his hands on me and I definitely didn't need my mom to see them either. She almost had a conniption fit when she saw the bruises on me when I returned home that night from the club. I had to stop her from calling the police. She even threatened bodily harm to Keyz, not that I blame her, I would react the same way if it was Keira.

"So, I'll see you on Friday."

He put his hand out for me to shake. "It was a pleasure doing business with you." I placed my hand in his and he caressed my

90

hand with his thumb. Warmth radiated from his huge hand and sparks flew from our hands to my now throbbing clit. I was fighting my attraction to him. Keyz had my heart, but my long neglected body yearned for a man's touch. It had been over four months since I was touched intimately.

Clearing my throat, I removed my hand and stepped back with a visible degree of discomfort. I didn't know how to feel about him stepping over the boundaries of professionalism. On one hand, his aggression at going after what he wanted turned me all the way on. It reminded me of Keyz and how he pursued me relentlessly. But on the other hand, I wasn't trying to go there with him or anyone else yet. "See you soon."

Dametrius took a step closer, but not invading my personal space again. "Since business is out the way, I would love to take you out to dinner."

I wanted to say yes because I could use some companionship from a man, but nothing about this man screamed friend. He would dominate me and my body if I gave him an opening. The thought of being dominated scared me, but excited me all at once. Even though I had only been with one man, I knew a man taking charge in the bedroom was something that got my juices flowing like a river. "I would love to, but I'm just getting out of a relationship and don't want to confuse anything with going on dates." I wouldn't mind going to dinner with him, but Keyz just killed my vibe and I was throwing the fuck you deuces to all men at this moment.

He smiled and licked his lips at the mention that I was no longer in a relationship. "The guy must have been a fool for letting you go."

Ignoring him, I said, "I'll see you soon," and walked to my car. I quickly hopped in and started backing out the driveway. When I looked forward, Dametrius was still standing there looking at me. Goodness, maybe I needed to go out with him and get dicked down. I wasn't ready for another man, but my body had other ideas. Or I could just call Keyz and use him for some dick, treating him like the hoe he was. If I did call Keyz and we were intimate, my resolve to move on would dissolve and we would be back together. There was no way Keyz would let me go if he got back in my bed.

Chapter 11

Some people will only "love you" as much as they can use you. Their loyalty ends where the benefits stop.

-Unknown

NeNe

A key being inserted into the lock alerted me that someone was trying to gain entry into my apartment. No one had a key except me and my man. I heard a soft rustling sound outside the door before the knob turned slowly and the door was pushed open. My man walked through the door. He had a hard look in his eyes. I was afraid of him when he looked like that. There was no reasoning with the monster that lurked beneath the surface.

"Hey baby, what are you doing here? I though you said we couldn't be seen together for a while because it would blow my cover?" I asked as he walked towards me.

He stalked towards me and grabbed my hair. "Did you say something to that bitch about the tape and them pictures?"

Danger coursed through my body as I stared into the cold, dead eyes of the man I loved. My body shivered, not in lust but in fear. I didn't understand why he was so mad at me. Everything he told me to, I did. He told me to lure Keyz into my bed, I did. Even when I got Keyz to screw me, I couldn't entrap him with a kid because he never finished inside me. I recorded us having sex and sent the video with the pictures like he told me to. I knew I messed up when I threw the video in Shaunie's face. My anger and hurt overrode my good sense. She got to be home with her man while I was stuck in between this game between my man and Keyz.

"No, I swear. I didn't say anything. When could I? We don't run in the same circles."

"I know yo ass lying. She mentioned the shit the other night at the club to Keyz." He shook me by the head as he spoke. Using my hair as an anchor, he pulled me closer to him. "You got feelings for that fuck nigga?"

I couldn't control the trembles that took over my body. Searching my mind for an answer to appease him, but drawing a blank, I said the only thing I could. "Baby, I love you. I don't care about her or Keyz. Everything I did, I did because you asked me to. Please let me go."

Just that quickly, he released me and stepped back. "Go upstairs and pack your shit. Keyz is going to come for you."

"For what?" I asked with a blank expression. Why would he come for me? Surely not over a video.

"For the damn video. It was taken inside your house of y'all fucking then sent to his girl."

"Yeah, so what. It ain't that big of a deal."

"You done played a role in fucking up his family. He gon' punish everybody involved. Since he only knows about you, he gon' punish you. He don't fuck around when it comes to Shaunie. Hurry up. If he catches up to you, you gon' be swimming with the 'gators."

I was green with envy when my man implied that Keyz would kill because someone caused his girl to leave him. Here I was, fucking a man on my man's order.

"Okay, let me pack a bag." Once inside my room, I began to panic. I grabbed my carry-on bag and began to stuff clothes inside. *What did I get myself into fucking with my man trying to set Keyz up?* I wasn't cut out for this duplicitous shit. Zipping my bag up, I turned to walk out the bedroom door and saw him standing there.

"I'm ready," I said with a shaky voice. He slowly approached me.

"I hate to do this, but I can't take a chance."

I stepped back. My heart began to pound and my knees felt weak. I knew what he meant. "I won't say anything, I swear. Don't do this. You told me you loved me. Please don't," I pleaded with him. My pleas got me nowhere because the look in his eyes didn't change. Until now, I never noticed how dead his eyes were. He showed no remorse as he advanced on me.

"I never loved you. I cared for you, but you are just a means to an end." His words stroked a firestorm of emotions. Hearing him say those words hurt me to the core. I did everything he had ever asked of me. My very soul was tainted from whoring myself for him and the beatings I took from him when something didn't go right and the beatings from Keyz when I was instructed to antagonize him as a distraction.

Wanting to lash out, but knowing he was getting ready to kill me, I looked around for something to use as a weapon, but couldn't find anything. Acting on impulse, I threw my carry-on bag at him and made a mad dash for the door, knocking down the floor lamp as I passed. I ran out the door and into the hall before he tackled me from behind. My body slammed against the wall, causing the framed pictures to fall and the glass to shatter. He tried to get on top of me when I turned over on my back, but I began to kick him as I tried to back my way to the living room.

"Stop. Please don't!" I screamed.

He grabbed my ankles and drug me to him. "I was gon' make it easy, but you just pissed me the fuck off." He picked out a shard of glass. My heart pounded even harder. It was hard to breathe.

I closed my eyes as he brought the glass down towards my body. My life flashed before my eyes. I knew I wasn't gon' make it out of here alive. When the glass pierced my flesh, I screamed in agony. The edges of the glass sliced out chunks of my skin, as he stabbed me repeatedly. He placed his hand over my mouth to stifle my screams. Tears leaked from my eyes. I bit his hand and let out an ear piercing scream when he removed his hand. He shoved the glass into my neck and that silenced any other screams. Blood poured from the gaping hole. I opened my eyes and stared at him, pleading with my eyes for him to stop. I gasped for air as I struggled to breathe. Emptiness filled me and I took a deep breath before permanently closing my eyes and letting the brilliant light engulf me.

Chapter 12

R.E.A.L. – Remember, everybody ain't loyal.

-Unknown

Keyz

Taking the black leather gloves from my back pocket, I placed them on before I pulled up the roll-up metal shutter that was over the warehouse door. The warehouse was a distribution facility that closed over ten years ago. I brought the place for little to nothing. Since I used this place for numerous criminal activities, I got it in an alias so it wasn't traced back to me. I stepped inside and disabled the alarm. The alarm was set with triggers attached to explosives to blow if it wasn't disabled in one minute upon entry. I wasn't taking no chances with my freedom. If by any chance the cops did raid the place, it would explode and level before anyone could get any evidence. Once I was done disabling the security, I enabled the surveillance around the warehouse.

Walking to the far end of the wall, I pushed the wall panel open. Behind the wall was a set of stairs that led to a basement I had built a few years back. Bouncing down the stairs, I walked over the metal shelves that held tools of torture and grabbed the scalpel. If Nene didn't give me the answers I wanted, then I was going to force them from her before I killed her. Bitch should have listened to my warning when I gave it. My heart was encased in ice for everybody except my family and moderation for a few friends. Everybody else could get it. The buzzer on the door alerted me that someone was outside. I looked on the surveillance monitor and saw Rayne coming, empty handed. *Where the fuck is NeNe?* I wondered as I pushed the buzzer to open the door for him.

I watched on the screen as he walked across the warehouse and down the stairs to the basement. His hard-soled shoes made a noise against the concrete floor.

"Yo, what it do? Where that package at?" I asked him when he walked into the room.

He walked over to me and dapped me up. "Man, someone already got to her. She was leaking from her throat. They left her ass on the floor."

I was glad the trouble-making hoe departed this life for the bullshit she pulled with my bae, but I was pissed someone got to her first. I had 99 problems, but she was no longer one.

"What happened?" My tone was sharp with frustration and it bled out with my words. We just planned the pick-up a few days ago.

Rayne shook his head. "When I went to pick the hoe up, the apartment door was cracked open. I went inside and signs of struggle was all through that bitch. Lamps were knocked over and pictures were knocked off the wall. She had clothes scattered over the bedroom."

Sounded like she was trying to run away until someone caught her. *I wonder how deep she was involved in this shit.* Not that I cared, because she forfeited her life the minute she came for me. "How long ago do you think it happened?"

"Bruh, couldn't have been long. The bitch wasn't stiff and her blood was still warm." Rigor mortis took between two and six hours to set in.

Fuck! Fuck! Fuck! We just missed getting her. "And you said the door wasn't kicked in, but cracked open."

"Yeah. Funny thing tho,' her living room area was fine. Everything was in place. Just the bedroom and the hallway was fucked up."

My hands clenched around the scalpel that I had in my hand. It was somebody she knew. "She let that nigga in. Which means she knew'em."

"I hate to say it, but I think that hoe may have been playing you the whole time. The timing all adds up. Plus, she in the center of the bullshit with Shaunie. I don't believe in coincidence, my nigga."

I didn't believe in coincidences either. This hoe was a distraction to keep me occupied and to cause issues in my relationship. Even tho' I cheated on my girl from time to time, everybody knew I dropped shit when it came to Shaunie. My only lead to anything was dead and I was back at square one. These niggas was one step ahead of me and the shit was fucking with me heavy. I wasn't a nigga accustomed to losing.

"Fuck! That hoe had some info."

"Nigga, you didn't think I was leaving that house emptied handed, did you?" Rayne asked holding up a bag with a smirk on his face.

Inside the bag was a bloody fingertip with a fire red nail. "Nigga, why the fuck you ain't been said something?" I snatched the bag from his hand.

"Nigga, you know I got to tell what happened before I get to the climax."

"Cool. Who you got in the lab to run the prints?"

He took the bag and tucked it back into his jeans. "Since we got rid of Briggs ass, it's gon' take me a minute to line up forensics on the finger."

I nodded my head. Before he turned on me, Briggs handled shit with his peeps on the inside, for a price. "Triple whatever they charge and tell them we need it asap."

"I got this," he said as my fist bumped.

"My nigga." Rayne had always been reliable, but my nigga was showcasing his skills.

I stood there for a minute contemplating my next moves. Staying ahead of the niggas after me and my team was imperative, so I had to strategize.

Putting my tools back on the shelves, I made sure everything was in its place. We walked back up the stairs to the main level and paused for me to set the alarm. I pulled down the metal door before we headed to our cars.

"Let me know as soon as we get word."

"I'm on it, my nigga," he said. He dapped me up before he climbed in his car.

Lately, Rayne had really been stepping up and staying on top of shit while I dealt with my personal issues. In my eyes, his loyalty was rock solid because fake niggas would have taken advantage of my distractions. I had to come up with something as a token of appreciation. If my niggas didn't stay loyal, they didn't stay alive long. But when my people showed loyalty to me, I took care of them.

Chapter 13

I believe in loyalty above everything. It's all or nothing with me.

-Unknown

Shaunie

Social shake-down on Q93 played over my radio inside my new house. It was Saturday night and me, Nikki and Stacy listened to the newest hit with the bounce beat as we unpacked my boxes, while drinking a few glasses of wine.

"That's the shit. Turn that up," Stacy said raising her head from her phone. Nikki walked over to the radio and turned the volume up. I raised my wine glass in the air and started twerking.

Nikki walked back over to us and started dancing. "Alright nah, Shaunie. Let me find out."

"Find out what, heifer?"

"Let me find out you done had one too many glasses and now you trying to get that D. Keyz would handle that for you," she said, teasing.

"Girl, whatever. I'm not even thinking of Keyz dirty dick ass. That's what I have a silver bullet for. Anyways, it ain't nothing for me to get some other D if I wanted. Dudes stay checking for me."

"Stacy, look at Shaunie talking sporty."

Stacy looked up from her phone. "I hear her talking that gangsta shit. She don't even look at other men." She went back to her phone like she had been for most of the night. Stacy was big on social media and stayed on Facebook, so I didn't mention why she was engrossed in her phone.

I playfully rolled my eyes at them. "Stacy, remember when we went to the club a while back and ole dude came to the bar and tried to buy me a drink."

"Bitch, niggas stay trying to buy drinks. I need particulars, boo boo."

"Ole dude with the dimples. He had the deepest dimples ever."

"Oh yes. Bay bae, he is hard to forget. He could get it."

"Well, he was my agent. He owns King's realty. When I tell you, when we met up to view houses, I thought he was gone throw me on the ground and take me right then and there." I fanned myself at the memory of how hot the sexual chemistry was between us.

"What happened?"

106

"He asked me out, but I said no. I'm just trying to focus on myself right now. I ain't gon' lie, I am sexually attracted to him though." Their mouths dropped opened at my declaration. I have only been with Keyz and had never uttered a word about wanting another man sexually. "Pick up your mouths, bitches. It isn't that serious."

Nikki recovered first. "I'm saying. That was shocking. I was speechless for a second. You know shit got to be real if it shuts my mouth."

"It's really not all that shocking. I never had any reason to mention another man. Keyz was all I needed, so why look?"

"How do you feel about this attraction to the guy?" Stacy asked.

My emotions over my new attraction were all over the place and I really couldn't pinpoint how to feel. "I'm confused. I just got out of a long-term relationship and I was deeply hurt. Shouldn't I be more concerned with getting back on track, instead of noticing other men?"

"Honey, the rose-tinted blinders are gone. It's normal to take notice of other men now that you are not consumed with Keyz."

"Plus, it feels good to know someone thinks I'm attractive. Not that Keyz didn't. It's just with the cheating, my self-confidence was knocked down a few notches, because I thought maybe I wasn't enough or was lacking something."

"Girl, please. Them niggas just thirsty for pussy. A bitch could fuck a man a hundred times a day. If they see something else and they like it, they gon' go for it, especially if the hoes are throwing it out there for them. That shit is all on them," Nikki said.

"I know that now. I'm just ready to move forward. New me and new house."

"Maybe a new man." Nikki lifted her eyebrow expectantly.

"Maybe. Now let's finish so we can go and get something to eat." The thought of opening myself up to anybody and being vulnerable again, almost made me have heart palpitations. I wasn't looking for a relationship. My last one almost destroyed me.

***

Once we were done unpacking, we hopped in Stacy's car and drove to the Waffle House on Read Boulevard. We grabbed our purses and headed inside. The place was packed, so we sat in the chairs and waited for a table. The waitress took us in the back where a table was available.

"Oh no the fuck he didn't," Nikki said before we reached the table. Her brows furrowed and she suddenly looked surprised.

Stacy and I looked at her. "What are you fussing about?" I asked her.

"Look in the motherfucking far left corner."

I did as she said and my eyes grew huge as saucers. Thugga was sitting across from some chick.

"That dirty nigga," I said. Grabbing Nikki's arm, I gave her a gentle squeeze as a show of support. Some people never learned. Thugga was still running around the city doing whatever the fuck he wanted with no regards to my friend. I was tired of watching her go through this same scenario over and over again. But until she was tired of it, there wasn't anything I could do.

"Nikki, bitch, I'm down for whatever," Stacy said.

"Y'all know what? I ain't even gon' clown. Fuck it. Imma eat my food and ignore his ass." She starting walking towards our table but stopped. "Who the fuck am I kidding? Y'all hoes know I can't let no shit like this go."

We followed her to the table where Thugga sat. It was about to go down. Nikki didn't usually care that she was in public.

"So, this how we do it now, Thugga? We post up in public with other bitches?" He didn't even acknowledge the chick. Thugga's eyes widened when he heard Nikki's voice. He looked from Nikki to the girl. I guess the cat had his tongue, because he couldn't say shit.

On the other hand, the chick didn't suffer from that problem. "Bitch, I am no one's bitch. You must not know who I am," the girl said.

"Who you is?" Nikki asked her.

"I'm...." the girl started, but didn't get to complete her sentence, because Nikki cut her off.

"Bitch, nobody cares and nobody knows. Keep your mouth closed while I talk to my man."

"If he is your man, why is he here with me?"

"Chill, Trina. You don't want none of that," Thugga said to the girl.

"Trina, so this the bitch that called your phone a while back and said y'all was fucking around." Thugga put his head down when he realized his mistake in saying the girl's name. He should have known Nikki wasn't going to forget a name. "You know what? Fuck you," she said and walked off.

Thugga got up and grabbed her wrist. "Nikki. wait…"

Nikki spun around, grabbed the fork off the table, and stabbed Thugga is the chest.

"Let my fucking hand go." She released her hold on the fork, but it stayed embedded in his chest.

The girl, Trina, jumped out of her seat, grabbed Nikki by her hair, and started hitting her. Stacy and I jumped in. When one fought, we all fought. We jumped her inside of Waffle House as Thugga stood by and watched. He didn't even remove the fork. Some of the customers looked like they wanted to stop us, but many seemed to enjoy the show. Many of them egged us on by yelling "ooohh."

We didn't stop beating her ass until she was on the floor. Nikki walked up to Thugga and smacked him in the face. He just rubbed his cheek while he stared at her.

"Fuck you and the bitch you with. Don't bother coming home. Try me if you want. I got a bullet with your name on it," she threatened him in front of everyone.

"Don't be saying no shit like that." Thugga grabbed her shoulders and shook her. Stacy and I stood watch to make sure the girl didn't get off the floor and try anything.

Nikki placed her hand over the hilt of the fork and pushed it further. "It's over for good this time. Stay the fuck away from me. I am not going to restrain my anger anymore at your disrespect. I am really going to hurt you." I didn't realize she had been holding her anger in check. Every time she found out Thugga cheated, she fucked him up.

She turned and walked away, but Thugga grabbed her wrist. "Wait, bae, I'm..," he said before she turned around, picked up a plate and hit him across the head. "Uuurgghh fuck! You had to do that, Nikki?" He didn't try hitting her back. Usually they would fight and go round for round, but I guess he knew he fucked up and she was tired of it.

"Damn, she fucked him up," one customer said in a loud whisper.

"Stay the fuck away from me, motherfucker. You want to fuck around? Well, now you are free to do what the fuck you want."

She stepped over the chick on the floor, like a piece of thrash, and walked out. I shook my head at Thugga before I followed her out. As we walked off, the girl, Trina, got up.

"How you gon' just stand there and let them jump me?" she asked Thugga.

"Bitch, is you serious? What you mean? That's my girl and my people. What you thought I was gon' help you? Bitch, please. I told your ass to shut up."

Trina huffed out a breath and shook her head as she gathered her things. "Niggas ain't shit," she mumbled before she stalked off to the restroom area.

As I walked out the door, distracted by what just happened, I collided with a hard chest. I looked up and came face to face with Dametrius. He had his arm wrapped around the shoulder of a girl that looked like she just came from the strip club. She had more skin exposed than she had covered. Already mad about the fight I just had, seeing him with a chick after he had been pushing up on me, just made me madder.

"Hey, Shaunie, how are you?" How could he ask me to dinner when he had a girl? I swear, these niggas just wasn't loyal.

"I'm good. Thanks for asking," I snapped at him. I shook my head at him and stepped past him and the girl. Before I made it to the car, I heard him calling my name as he jogged towards me. The girl walked behind him. I turned around and folded my arms. "What it is?"

"What you walk off with an attitude for?" He stepped closer, invading my personal space.

"Back up away from me. I don't need your girlfriend coming over here with no foolishness." I pushed his hard chiseled chest.

He grabbed my wrist in a firm hold. Not enough to hurt, but to stop me from pushing him.

"She isn't my girlfriend." He turned to the girl. "Damara, come here."

The girl rolled her eyes before walking towards us. "What, Dam?"

"Shaunie, this is my sister, Damara. Damara, this is the woman I was telling you about."

"Oh, so you are the Ms. Shaunie Williams my brother can't stop talking about. Nice to meet you." She put out her hand for me to shake.

"Nice meeting you." Now self-conscious at my dishevel appearance, I made an attempt to fix my clothes and used my fingers to comb out my hair.

She turned back to her brother. "I'll get us a table."

When she walked away, Dametrius looked at me. "What were you saying about my girlfriend?" he asked with a cocky smile. "You have to know I'm feeling you. Don't turn me down a third time. Let me take you out."

I was about to refuse, until I looked up and saw Thugga walk out the door with that trick, Trina. Seeing him and the girl reminded me of my own failed relationship. Fuck it. Since niggas wanted to step out and play, I was going to play, too.

"I would love it if you did."

"Cool, I'll call you tomorrow." He grabbed my hand, brought it to his lips and placed a kiss to my knuckles. I felt Thugga staring intently at me the whole time. Yeah, nigga, now go run and tell that to Keyz.

Chapter 14

I learned the real meaning of love. Love is absolute loyalty.

-*Sylvester Stallone*

Keyz

"Yo, ma. Where y'all at?" I yelled when I walked through the door of my mama's house. I walked into the living room, looking for her and my kids. When I didn't find them in the living room, I headed back towards the play room. The sounds of laughter and giggling could be heard in the backyard, so I went outside.

"What's up, y'all?" I asked them. My mom was sitting on the patio chair and the kids were playing on the trampoline.

When my kids saw me, they climbed off and ran to me. "Daddy, Daddy," Keira and Shaun screamed, simultaneously. I bent down, picked up my princess, and kissed her cheek.

My son put out his fist for a pound. "What up, lil' man?"

"Nothing, showing my sister how to jump while we wait on you," Shaun said. As much as I hated what I put Shaunie through, I was glad my secret was finally out. I wanted my kids to have a good relationship. Shaun was a good big brother.

"Y'all go play for a minute while I talk with your grandma."

When I tried putting Keira down, she started to cry.

"No, daddy. Hold me." She placed her arms around my neck and squeezed. Keira had been real attached to me since Shaunie moved out. She hated for me to leave her sight.

"I'm not going anywhere, baby girl. Daddy's right here," I said as I patted her back and kissed her head.

Shaun walked up to her with his hands out. "Come on, KeKe. Let's go play." Keira leaned over and went to her brother.

I watched them play together for a few minutes before I turned to my mom. "Hey ma," I leaned over and kissed her cheek.

"Don't 'hey ma' me. I'm steaming mad right now."

I sighed. It was always something with her. "What you mad for now?"

"I don't like that Ashley. She is a disrespectful ass trick." My mama pursed his lips like she ate something distasteful. Ashley's behavior and personality could leave a nasty taste in anyone's mouth. "She dropped of Shaun and didn't bother to get out of the car. I don't like her," she completed with an eye and head roll.

Personally, I didn't care if she got out the car or not, as long as she dropped my son off. After the incident at her house, I stopped going over there and I told her she had to drop Shaun off at my mama's house. "Imma tell her about it."

"You better. I ain't got no problem checking her ass. The next time she come over, Imma be waiting outside to tell that slut bucket about herself. Fuck wrong with her."

My mama was going in on Ashley. "Damn, ma. You that heated 'cause she didn't get out the car?"

"No. I don't like the home-wrecking bitch. I love my grandson, but I don't respect no hoe that goes after another woman's man."

"Ma, I know you mad, but please don't talk about Ashley in front of Shaun."

She gave me a look that caused me to squirm in my chair. "I ain't fucking down bad like that, I would never. I should slap your ass for that."

"Man, chill with all that, damn."

She grabbed her drink off the table and leaned back in her chair. "It's a damn shame you beefing with both of your baby mamas. You got to pick up both your kids from over here. Not that I blame Shaunie."

At the mention of Shaunie's name, a wave of longing washed over me. I missed waking up to her and seeing her smile. I missed making love to her. She refused to talk to me about anything but our daughter. My family was slipping right through my hands.

"How is she?" I knew she was fine. I hired two bodyguards to split the twenty four shift to watch over her and my seed. With shit heating up in the streets and me not knowing who was behind my spots getting hit, I wasn't taking any chances with my family. Now that we weren't living under the same roof, I didn't want niggas to grow balls and try to hurt me by going for my weak spot. They reported back to me everything she did. Including that little stunt outside the Waffle House with a nigga a few days ago.

"She looking real good. You know, trying to move on and shit. I told her to try them dating sites." My forehead creased and I narrowed my dark eyes in apparent anger.

"Is you fucking serious?" I jumped out my chair with my hands clenched. *How could she even suggest some shit like that?* I thought.

She smirked at me. "You mad or nah?" She antagonized me, deliberately, by bringing up Shaunie with other men. "You didn't want her when you had her. She deserves happiness." The anger drained from me just that quickly.

I sat back down in my chair and put my head in my hand. "I always wanted her. I fucked up. We were young when we settled down and maybe I wasn't truly ready to commit to one woman. I thought I was missing out on something. My ego grew big when I knew I could tag any woman I wanted. The chase was a thrill." My mom was quiet as she listened to my reasons for the things I did.

She placed her hand on my back and rubbed. "Baby, I love you and I want you to be happy. I know you love Shaunie, but you have to give her time to come to terms with everything that happened. Hell, she may never come to terms, but whatever she decides that's a decision you have to live with. For every action there is a reaction. Her leaving you is the consequences of your actions."

Nodding my head, I stood up. I didn't need to sulk today while I had my kids, even though I knew what she said was the truth.

"Alright. We going. I promised to take the kids to the toy store and to get some ice cream. We'll see you later."

"Shaun, Keira. Come gave me a kiss before y'all go," my mom called to the kids.

They ran to her and kissed her cheek. "Bye, grandma." Shaun hugged her and stepped back. When Shaun was first introduced to my mom and uncle a few weeks back, he was very hesitant and took a few visits to warm up to them. Now, he fit seamlessly into my family like he had known them all his life. The transition had been smooth for him. I was thankful that he was finally a part of my family like he deserved. One of my biggest regrets was keeping him a secret.

"Bye, maw maw. Love you," Keira said.

"Bye Shaun, Tootles KeKe," my mom told them.

"Tootles, maw maw," my daughter said blowing a kiss at my mama before she launched herself onto my legs with her hands up.

Shaun grabbed my hand once I picked up Keira. Me and my kids left my mama's house to spend the day together as a family. Only one missing was Shaunie. Then my family would be complete.

Chapter 15

I look for these qualities and characteristics in people. Honesty is number one, respect, and absolutely the third would have to be loyalty.

-Summer Altice

Shaunie

My girls and I decided to do some retail therapy to relieve ourselves of the stress the last few days caused. Stacy and Killer were beefing because she wanted a baby and he didn't. I saw the yearning in her eyes every time she looked at our kids. Thugga refused to move out the house this time, so him and Nikki had been fighting just about every day. His behavior disgusted me how he refused to leave when he was the one in the wrong. I knew he stayed hoping she would just let the Waffle House situation go. He should have at least left until she had time to cool off and make some decisions. All the arguing and fighting wasn't endearing him to her.

Keyz had been blowing up my phone about me and Dam talking outside of the Waffle House. I knew Thugga's cheating ass was going to flap his gums like a bitch. Niggas gossiped like hoes.

Keira sat in her stroller playing with her iPad while Nikki, Stacy, and Lil' Corey walked beside us.

"So what are you going to do, Nikki?" I asked her.

"Since he won't get out, I'm leaving. I'll start looking for a place tomorrow."

"That's fucked up that he refused to leave. I mean damn, he got caught red-handed. Man up and get the fuck out," Stacy said. Something was bothering her. I was going to talk to her later about it. She usually was the level-headed one.

"Y'all can come stay by me. My new place has enough space. I could use the company," I told Nikki. I was feeling lonely in my house with just me and Keira. This was the first time I had ever lived alone. I went from my parent's house to a house with Keyz. My new house felt empty, void, the way a house feels when a complete family didn't occupy the space. Someone from the family was missing.

"Girl, I think I might. Thugga keep playing with me and Imma go to jail. For real."

"Well, bitch, I got your bail," I told her with a laugh.

124

We walked inside BeBe and looked at the dresses. Keyz blowing up my phone and hounding me was not going to stop me from going on my date. I was looking for a cute little dress that was both sexy and sophisticated. After grabbing a few dresses I liked, I went inside of the dressing room while Stacy watched Keira and tried on a red halter dress first. The dress molded to my curves like a second skin. I stepped out the dressing room to show Nikki.

"What do you think?" I twirled so they could see the full dress.

"Uuumm. I like it. It has the right amount of *come freak me by eating me and you could get it, but not right now.* Know what I mean?" Nikki said.

Laughing, I went back inside the dressing room, took off the dress, and put my clothes back on. Yeah, I knew just what she meant. Lil' Corey ran to me and his mom when he saw us leave the dressing room. Pushing the stroller, Stacy followed him and we all headed to the register to check out. When we got to the register, Keira bounced excitedly in her seat when she spotted Shaun standing next to his mom and another chick. Ashley smirked at me, but remained quiet. Her smugness wafted from where she stood and it was hard to not feel it. I didn't know if she felt some type of victory because she played a part in breaking apart my family or me losing my job. Either way, I didn't care and wasn't worried over her. I refused to further feed into the insecurities that were triggered by Keyz' cheating. So I wasn't going to start the questioning game where I asked myself how could he cheat on me for someone who wasn't prettier or smarter. It wouldn't make a difference if she was, because the pain would have been the same. He would have cheated anyway, because that's what he wanted to do. She wasn't a threat to me. The hoe couldn't even fight.

I looked at her and wondered what Keyz saw when he looked at her. Did he desire her? It was hard for me to see how. She looked like a bucket of fuck. Her weave was cheap looking, her clothes were thotish, and her shoes wasn't red bottoms, but some knock off look-a-likes of the ones I got two seasons ago. I shook my head at her poor appearance, at least to my standards. This broad wanted to be a *silver platter hoe,* but didn't know that silver tarnishes. Label me a woman, because I wasn't trying to be a silver platter hoe, a dime, a Barbie, or a bad bitch, because I wasn't tarnished, a coin, or a child's toy.

"Sha, Sha." Keira dropped her iPad and held out her arms for him. I bent down to get her iPad, but really needed a second to compose myself and fix my face, so I didn't show any weakness in front of Keyz' baby mama. It was still hard for me to think of Shaun, less on seeing him.

Shaun walked over to her, hugged her and kissed her cheek. "Hey, Keke." His interaction with my baby caused the ice to melt around my heart a little. Even a blind person could see the brother and sister had a good bond. He turned around and walked up to Lil' Corey. "What's up, cuz?" he asked as he fist pounded him, obviously imitating his dad.

"Chilling, cuz. We going to shoot hoops Saturday. You coming?" Lil' Corey asked him.

"My dad said he was picking me up, so yeah." The kids had an entire conversation as if we weren't even there. My girls and I mean mugged Ashley and her friend the whole time. I looked her up and down, not bothering to hide my disdain. She looked like a cheap imitation of Rihanna with her red hair. Trap was written all over her. Or should I say thot with her thot dots in her face. Cheek piercings dominated her face. The cashier's attention was riveted on us, like she was waiting for a scene to play out in front of her. I didn't want to clown in front of the kids, but if she jumped she would get checked. I was truly surprised that Nikki held her tongue.

He finally looked up at me with a hesitant expression. "Hey, Ms. Williams," he said and his mom smacked her teeth loud enough that it echoed throughout the store. I wanted to tell that trick bitch something, but I was trying to be mindful of the kids. My heart seized up when he looked at the floor, breaking eye contact with me. I didn't know if people had been talking in front of him, but he clearly knew some of the situation. He never used to act like this around me.

"Hey, Shaun," I said. Quickly thinking of something to break the awkward silence between us. "How is school?"

He looked up and smiled. "It's okay. The kids keep asking for you. I told them your baby was my sister."

I cringed at the thought that I was still a topic at the school. "That's awesome," I choked out. "Well, we have to get going. Keira tell Shaun bye." She waved at Shaun before Stacy turned the stroller around. I placed the dress on the counter, turned to Ashley. "Bitch," I muttered. Anger darkened her face, but what the fuck. I didn't give a shit. I walked and made sure to turn my swag on, because I knew she was looking. Bitch may have had a baby by my man and fucked him a time or two, but I was still *that* bitch.

***

"So that's Keyz' baby mama, huh?" Stacy asked once we all sat down. We decided to get something to eat from the food court in the mall. The encounter didn't bother me as much as I thought it would.

I placed my baby's food in front of her. "Yep. That's Ashley's home-wrecking ass. You know what? I am not going to spend another minute worrying over Keyz, his hoes, or his baby mama. I can't move on unless I get over the shit."

"Boo, I hear ya and feel ya. It's time I get serious about leaving Thugga. He ain't gon' change. It's best I leave before I have to deal with a baby mama. With all the cheating he do, it's a surprise I haven't yet. No offense, Shaunie."

"None taken. Cheaters are going to cheat. I can't stand a cheater," I said. Pain etched Stacy's features at my remark. Her sadness was palpable and it flooded over us. She put her head down and I heard soft sniffles and saw her shoulders shaking. "Stacy, what's wrong?" I asked her. I sat my drink down and scooted closer to her in the booth.

She lifted her head slowly and began to fumble with the napkin. "I cheated on Killer," she said in a soft voice choked with emotions. I quickly looked at Lil' Corey to see if he was paying attention to us. He had earplugs in his ears playing with his iPad while he ate his food. Keira was busy eating nuggets.

An uncomfortable silence filled the table. I didn't know how to respond to the bomb she just dropped on us. She saw the drama, heartache, and pain Nikki and I were going through because of someone's unfaithfulness. It felt like a slap in the face.

"How could you?" I asked her with condemnation dripping from my voice. I didn't mean to sound that way, I just couldn't fathom how she did it. She always talked about how much she loved Killer. Love didn't let a person cheat or hurt the ones they claimed to love.

"See, that's why I didn't want to tell y'all. I knew y'all would judge me."

"Well, you should have kept that shit to yourself," I snapped at her. I knew I was taking out my anger on her, but I couldn't seem to stop myself. I hated that I sounded so self-righteous, but my pain exploded to the surface.

"Now wait a minute, chill Shaunie. Her situation ain't your situation. Hear her out," Nikki said.

Stacy looked at Nikki with an expression of gratitude. "Please don't judge me. It happened. I'm not perfect."

I sat there in a moment of moral indecision. Stacy was my friend and I loved her. However, I wanted no part or knowledge of knowing someone was cheating on their mate. The wan countenance of my friend forced me to stay and hear her out. "Okay." I scooted away from Stacy and moved closer to Keira.

"So, what happened?" Nikki asked.

"Me and Killer had a huge fight about a month ago. We were fighting about a baby again. I told him I wanted a baby and he refused. He said if I kept pressing the issue, he was going to leave." She paused and got quiet as if her mind was replaying the scene. A lone tear fell down her cheek. "I was upset when I went to work and the doctor I work with walked in on me crying. He comforted me and in my vulnerable state I allowed him to kiss me and one thing led to another. It only happened once, but it's eating me up inside. I want to tell Killer, but I'm scared he will use this to leave me. I just want a baby to complete our family. Is that so bad?"

Once again, silence descended around the table at her explanation. "I'm sorry I jumped down your throat without hearing you out first. I appreciate you being there in my time of need. I am going to give you the only advice I can. Honesty is the best policy. If you don't 'fess up to him and he finds out, you probably will

131

lose him anyway." I grabbed my daughter from out the highchair and left them at the table. My conscience wouldn't allow me to stay and listen to anything more. "I love you and I am here for you as always about anything, but I don't what or need to hear the details. I'm so sorry, but I just don't want no part in knowing. My loyalty is to you, so whatever you decide, I will support you." Being on the receiving end of deception had left me with little to no tolerance for it from people who surrounded me.

Chapter 16

Unless you can find some sort of loyalty, you cannot find unity and peace in your active living.

-Josiah Royce

Keyz

"Tell me the numbers. It better be what I want to hear," I said to my soldiers. It was our monthly meeting and every nigga who ran one of my spots was responsible for reporting to me their intake figure, even tho' Rayne already told me since he counted the money. Everyone on my team had a job. As the boss, I couldn't do everything, so I delegated to niggas I trusted or who proved their loyalty to the team.

The meeting was being held at one of the many houses that I had. The location of the meeting changed every month and was only revealed thirty minutes before the appointed time. That way niggas couldn't drop the dime on us. We sat around a ten chair oblong table and more chairs were up against the wall. The room and everybody in it had already been swept for bugs and wires and the walls were soundproof.

"The profit on trap Freret Street tripled since I took over that spot as sergeant. I keep the workers stacked with goods and the spot is open for re-up twenty four seven, with call in appointments at two hour intervals, where I meet them away from the house to keep the heat off. I know previously the workers came to the house to pick up product, but that shit was a travesty. We may as well just write dope house on the door, the way Boobie had the fiends and workers hanging around," said Hassan. He was a cat that used to work the corners, but I had been watching him for a while. I liked how he operated and handled himself in the streets. He reminded me of myself the way he handled shit like a boss and Rayne the way he thought shit out. My insight to put him on and take over a trap was dead on.

"That's what's up. The rest of y'all can take a page from that lil' nigga's books and increase the profits," I said as I looked around the room at the other sergeants. The one's who looked away were well aware of the fact that the reprimand was directed at them. My eyes landed on Chris at the other end of the table. He ran the trap on Esplanade Avenue. "Tell me Chris, how is the numbers for the spot?"

He fidgeted in his seat, then stopped and looked up at me. "The numbers are steady," he said nervously. I gave him a glare to let him know I knew he was lying. Rayne reported numbers to me weekly.

I leaned back in my chair and tapped my jaw with my forefinger. "Is that right?" I asked with narrowed eyes and a voice full of doubt and accusation.

"We could be doing better at the spot, but the clientele been dry," he attempted to backtrack and get himself out of the hole he dug, now that I called him on his shit.

At my head nod, Thugga got up from the table, walked to the TV that was mounted on the wall and inserted a DVD. Everyone in the room remained quiet as the video played the discriminating evidence against Chris. The video showed workers going to the trap house to re-up product and Chris turning them away while he was busy using my trap house as a fuck pad. He had several different hoes going in and out.

I pressed the button on the remote to turn it off, then I stood up and walked slowly towards the other end of the table.

"One thing I hate, is a liar. If I can't trust you to tell the truth about simple shit, how can I trust you with complicated shit?" I asked him as I took out my pocket knife from my front pocket and ran the tip along by finger. "But the main thing I hate is when niggas fuck with my money."

Chris leaned forwarded and placed his hands on the table. "Keyz, man I fucked…." he said right as I brought the knife down and stabbed him in the hand with it so hard, the knife went through the table. I leaned my weight into the knife and twisted it. Blood squirted from his hand and leaked from the hole. I felt the blade hitting the bones in his hand.

"Never bite the hand that feeds you," I whispered in his ear. I pulled the knife out and he screamed. Again, I brought the knife down causing him to flinch in expectation of being stabbed again, but I wiped my knife on his shirt before I flipped it close and put it back in my pocket. Chris' shoulders sagged in relief for a minute. "Thugga, finish him off." He began to beg and plead for leniency, but his pleas fell on deaf ears.

Everyone watched in silence as Thugga pulled his gun from the waistband of his jeans and instructed Chris to get up and walk to the bathroom. At the realization that he was going to the bathroom, Chris fervently renewed his pleas. Everyone in the room knew that when someone was instructed to go into the bathroom, they didn't return. After the execution, their bodies are eaten away by acid until nothing was left. As Chris was led away, despite his pleading, the vibe in the room stiffened further and an uncomfortable silence fell.

I walked back to my seat and sat down. My elbows rested on the table as I clasped my hands together with my fingertips touching. "I will not tolerate any more bullshit from this crew. One more slip up or fuck up and Imma wipe out this motherfucker. Permanently. So, you motherfuckers better start becoming your brother's keeper. We are a fucking team, so we need to work like one. There are no I's or he's on the team. If a nigga fucking up, check him. Now, you niggas know I'm the type of nigga that's gon' make sure when I eat, y'all eat. Let's kill the bullshit. No more warnings." I looked every nigga in the eye to let them know I meant fucking business.

"Now that that is settled, anything else we need to talk about? If any of y'all have something you need to bring to the table, now is the time." I paused. "Good job with the numbers. Let's keep the dead presidents coming in so we can all get paid. Meeting adjourned." We all began to make our way outside. Some of the crew congregated and shot the breeze about shit that was happening around the hood, while some of the others walked away with their mouths set in a hard line and stiff shoulders. But I didn't feel any shade from anybody over the events that happened in the meeting.

The crew walked ahead as me, Killer, Qwan, Thugga, and Rayne trailed the rear end. Most were so busy talking with each other or on their phones, that they didn't notice the three black cars coming up the street until they skidded to a halt and opened fire. Quickly springing into action, we took cover behind our cars and returned fire. I shot out the tires of two of the vehicles, before I started aiming at the shooters. Niggas usually shoot then pull off. I wanted answers, so I jeopardized their possible escape by blowing out the tires.

The sounds of gunfire lit up the night air in the mostly vacant area. The shoot-out lasted for about five minutes with constant trigger play from both sides. After the vehicle in the front took off, members from my crew lit up the remaining vehicles, until no return fire was heard. I saw Hassan cautiously approach one of the vehicles. When he opened the door, the driver was slumped over the steering wheel. Rayne moved towards the cars and checked the other man. While he did that, I surveyed the damage done to my team. Surprisingly, especially since we were out in the open, we only had minor injuries, but no fatalities. I was low-key proud as fuck of my crew. They stood up and handled business like G's.

"Yo, we got one that's breathing," Hassan called out.

Killer quickly walked over to pump another bullet in him, but I walked over and pushed his hand aside. *Fuck this nigga in a hurry for?* I thought. Sure enough, the nigga was gasping for breath. "Rayne, call doc and give him the location to the warehouse. Tell him to get there in ten minutes." I turned around and pointed at two dudes. "Y'all niggas get his half dead ass in the SUV. Apply pressure to that hole in his stomach. I want that nigga to live by any means necessary. Give his ass CPR if you have to." The nigga was my only link to whoever was behind this shooting. Since dead men couldn't talk, I wanted this nigga to live like I wanted some of my bae's pussy. Maybe all this bullshit could be put to rest with the answers he could supply. Everyone followed orders quickly so we could hurry up and get ghost before someone took notice of the disturbance the shoot-out caused and alerted the authorities.

Rayne walked up to me. "The doc is on his way."

"Cool. Drive the SUV to the warehouse. Imma text you the security code. Put the code in within a minute. Don't let anyone else in, but the doc. Keep your eye on him at all times," I instructed him.

He dapped me up. "I got this." I walked off. My dick was hard from the possibility of finding out who was responsible for these hits. It was going to be lights out for any nigga whose name came up.

Chapter 17

Loyal women deserve the best.

-Unknown

Shaunie

I gave my keys to the valet to park my car and went inside the restaurant. Dametrius and I decided to meet up at the restaurant instead of us riding together. Being with Keyz for several years taught me to be cautious when letting people know where I lay my head. As I walked up to the hostess area, my stomach filled with butterflies. I had never been on a date with another guy other than Keyz. "I'm with the King party," I told the hostess with a polite smile.

"Right this way, Ms. Williams," the hostess said. I followed behind her as she escorted me to the table where Dametrius sat.

When he saw me, he stood up. "Hello, gorgeous. You look beautiful," he greeted me as he took my hand and kissed it. He pulled out a chair for me.

I knew I was looking good. I wore the red halter dress I purchased the other day with gold strappy Chanel scandals. My hair was bone straight and I applied some light makeup to top it off. I was flawless. "Thank you," I said as I sat in the chair. I fiddled anxiously with the strap of my purse. Nervousness caused butterflies to take flight in my stomach. My experience with men, with the exception of Keyz, was pretty much non-existent. I interacted with some of his friends and associates, but even that was limited.

The waiter came over, took our orders, and came back a few minutes later with our drinks.

"So, you know what I do for a living. Would you mind if I asked you what you do?" Dametrius asked me.

I took a sip of my wine before I answered. "I'm a certified teacher. I taught kindergarten."

"Taught?"

"Yes. I took some time off for personal reasons. Now I'm interested in opening a daycare."

"That's cool. Let me know when you are ready and I can help you find a location if you like."

Since we crossed the line of professionalism by going on a date, I definitely wouldn't deal with him when I was ready to get a building. "Maybe," I replied without committing to it.

Midway through the meal, the personal questions began. I really liked his vibe, so I didn't mind the questions as long as they didn't become too personal.

"Do you have any kids?" I asked him.

Shaking his head, he wiped his mouth with his napkin. "No, I don't have any kids. I wouldn't disrespect my future wife like that."

My eyebrow lifted upwards at his response. I was expecting an affirmative. "Why do you say that? How is it disrespectful to have kids prior to marriage?" After a response like that, I really wanted to know how and why he saw it that way. My mother instilled in me the importance of waiting until marriage, but shit happens.

"It's disrespectful, because then she would have to deal with a baby mama and a child under her roof that isn't hers. Females nowadays don't have no chill. They don't respect boundaries. Baby mamas be quick to use the child as a bargaining chip to try and control the man. I'm not about to just be planting my seed any and everywhere. I don't want my lady to deal with no bullshit like that. Plus, I want all my seeds under my roof. Now, I ain't judging nobody. That's my personal choice. To each their own."

He said all the right words. I would be lying if I said they didn't have me feeling some kind of way. I couldn't help but respect a man who had that mentality about not spreading his seeds far and wide. "That's very interesting. And I must say, spot on. Working in my field, I saw a lot of kids without fathers. If a father was present, they usually had so much drama to deal with from their baby mama."

"So, what about you? Do you have any kids?"

I smiled as I thought about my daughter. "Yes. I have a daughter. She's two."

"And what about her father?

Choosing my words carefully, I paused before I spoke. "We recently separated." Pain pierced my tattered heart at the thought of my separation from Keyz. I was trying to move on, but my heart had other plans. *Will I forever miss him?* I asked myself.

"Well. He couldn't be me. I would do everything in my power to keep a beautiful woman like you."

His words evoked my lust like a match to a flame. I crossed my legs and tightened them. "Um, thank you." I veered the conversation away from anything else personal. Confusion was a riot in my mind and heart because I wrestled with loneliness from missing the other piece of my heart and my lust for Dametrius.

We continued to talk throughout our meal. He stimulated my mind, because he was able to hold his own during the conversation as we talked about politics, the economy, and religion. For the first time, I admitted my sexual attraction to him, at least to myself, and I allowed the feeling to wash over me.

After dinner, we walked outside of the restaurant to the valet area. Dametrius placed his hand at the small of my back as we walked. I gave my ticket to the valet and he left to retrieve my car. Dametrius and I were the only ones outside. I turned to him and smiled. "I had a really great time tonight. Thank you."

He grabbed my hands. "The pleasure was all mine, gorgeous. I would really love it if you would allow me to take you out again."

"I think I could arrange that," I said flirtatiously. For several heartbeats, we stared into each other's eyes. He palmed my cheek, tilted his head towards me, and placed a soft kiss to my lips. I hesitantly parted my lips to allow his tongue entry when his swiped over my lips. My breath caught in my throat as desire flooded me, leaving my juices to drip in my panties. He pressed closer, demanding for me to allow his tongue entry into my mouth, deepening the kiss. I was lost as his mouth consumed mine.

My response to him shocked me. His hand on my cheek felt different then Keyz' touch. The taste of his tongue was different. Every sensation from Dametrius was different from Keyz,' but pleasant all the same.

The sound of an engine roaring, interrupted our first kiss. Dametrius stepped back. "Shaunie," he murmured my name like it was a life line.

The kiss was so sweet and sensual, it took me a moment to get my equilibrium. "Thank you for such an amazing night." I looked up at him and blushed at the hunger in his yes.

The valet pulled up in my car and stepped out. I walked to my car with Dametrius right behind me. I got inside my car and he leaned over and placed a quick, chaste kiss to my lips.

"I couldn't resist just one more taste," he said as he stepped back and closed my car door. We smiled at each other through the window. I felt like a school girl with her first crush as I drove off.

***

The first thing I noticed when I walked in the door after dropping Keira off to Ms. Lynn's house was the boxes stacked up in the foyer. I walked in the living room and found Nikki watching TV on the sofa.

"Girl, what is in all of those boxes?" I asked as I sat on the sofa and removed my heels. I had been ripping and running all day with my agent, looking for the perfect building for my daycare center.

"That's my stuff from the house. I had to go and pack up a lil' something something after I dropped Lil' Thugga off at Thugga's mama," she said with an evil smirk on her face.

I placed my hand on my hip and tilted to the side. "A lil' something, huh? Look like you packed up the whole house."

She laughed and rolled her eyes. "Bitch, I pretty much did. I swear I was Petty Betty in that motherfucker. I took the dishes, batteries from the remote, pillows, towels, soap. Bitch, if I bought it, I took it. Hell, if I thought I bought it, I took it." Nikki grabbed the remote off the end table and turned the TV off. "The food got thrown in the garbage can without a bag, because I took the garage bags, too. I hope he don't have to take a shit, because I gots the Charmin toilet paper in that box right there," she said, pointing to the box next to the loveseat.

This bitch was as crazy as they came. Who the fuck does all that? "Well, bitch, did you at least get you and Lil' Thugga's clothes?"

"Fuck clothes. I got that nigga's Black Card. I could buy us some more clothes."

We burst out laughing. Only Nikki would say that. Even though we had different personalities, we got along so well. I would trade everything to keep her in my corner. Her loyalty was unwavering to everyone she loved, which could be a bad thing if that same loyalty wasn't returned. Her unwavering loyalty to Thugga is what allowed her to stay and deal with his bullshit for so long.

"How was your date the other day?" she asked me. It had been three days since my date. Dam and I talked every night.

A huge smile spread on my face. "It was so nice just going out and talking. We talked about everything. He is such as gentleman and intelligent, too. I'm feeling him."

"Well, I'm glad for you. You deserve some happiness. I'm about to find me a lil' trade. Thugga's ass has been cancelled for good this time around. My loyalty can only go so far."

"I hear that." We both got quiet, lost in our thoughts. My heart still yearned for Keyz, but I was beginning to think our time together had passed. It was time for me and Nikki to let loose the shackles that our loyalty bonded us to like slaves. Our loyalty for the men we loved caused us plenty of drama and bullshit. Unconditional love and loyalty shouldn't hurt. Loyal women deserved the best.

Chapter 18

Loyalty – Loy-al-ty (loi-uhl-tee) noun. The state or quality, or an instance of being loyal; faithfulness to commitments or obligations.

-Merriam Webster

Keyz

Scrolling through my phone, I checked for a message from Shaunie as I sat on the bench in the park watching Shaun and Keira play. She had been ducking and dodging me, since I called and went off on her about her supposed date with some high yellow ass fuck nigga. When her bodyguard called and reported her lil' make out session in front of a restaurant, I almost jumped in my car, drove to the place, and shot that nigga on the spot, then beat her ass. Just thinking about the shit had me heated. I was tired of waiting for a response from her, so I sent another text.

Me: I know yo ass saw my message.

She didn't reply to any of my previous messages, but this time I got an immediately response. I bet the only reason she responded this time is because I had Keira.

My Bae: What do you want Keyon?

Me: Let me come through and eat on that pussy.

A nigga ain't had no pussy in almost five months. I been jerking off for so long and often, I think I got carpal tunnel. It wasn't that I couldn't get no pussy from bitches. The pussy I wanted ain't want to have shit to do with me on that level. My change in heart about creeping around had nothing to do with Shaunie not fucking with me. Okay, I'm lying, that's a part of it. Everything I needed was always at home waiting for me. She was my better half. Niggas would give their left nut for a chick like her and there I was fucking over her with random bitches that didn't mean shit. If I ever got her back, I wasn't ever letting go. A bitch couldn't get me to fuck her if her pussy was dripping with gold.

My Bae: Boy bye with that bullshit. You can't even smell the pussy let alone eat it.

Me: Y you playing? What the fuck is wrong with you?

My Bae: I'm not playing. You refuse to listen when I say I moved on.

Me: If you mean moving on with that fuck nigga then you can forget about that shit. Yo ass better dead that shit like yesterday.

My Bae: Don't call or text me unless it's about Keira.

My hand clenched the phone and I almost threw it out of anger. I was getting tired of begging and pleading with Shaunie's ass. I knew I fucked up and she needed time, but my patience was running thin. I was missing my girl and needed her. I half-way thought about going to her house and dragging her ass back home, but I dismissed that thought, because I wanted her to come back on her own. I put my phone in my pocket and watched Shaun push Keira on the swing. My baby girl loved being with her brother. Their relationship is the best thing that came from the drama I put my family through.

A woman with a small dog sat on the bench next to me and I looked at her from the side. She was just my type too or should I say she resembled Shaunie. Light-skinned, petite, and long black hair. Her face was cute, but not drop dead gorgeous.

"Are those your kids?" she asked me as she settled on the bench. She sat her handbag on the bench between us.

"Yeah, those my younguns," I answered without looking at her. I looked at the street, checking my surroundings. With all the shit I had been up in the last few days, a nigga couldn't be too careful. My bodyguard was standing some ways back just peeping game, making sure a nigga didn't try to run up. Usually, I didn't keep myself surrounded with guards. Imma hood nigga and I likes to handle my own. Since the last shoot out, I kept a guard or two around when I had my kids.

The chick bent down to pat her dog and I followed her movement. "They are so cute. I love seeing men with their kids. It's so sweet."

I looked at her ass when she bent over. The top of her ass cheeks were poking out the top of her shorts. My dick started swelling at the sight of her plump flesh, but immediately went flaccid. I was trying not to fuck anymore hoes. Plus, I wasn't trying to give Shaunie's stubborn ass a reason to not come back home. If she found out I was fucking with another hoe, she would take that much longer to come back.

"Thanks, ma." I leaned back, put my arm on the back of the bench, and watched my kids play. I didn't have no time for bitches and their thirst traps.

She turned to me with a dazzling smile on her face. My eyes dipped down to her breasts. Shaunie's titties looked better.

"I'm Trinesha," she said as she put her hand out.

Lifting my eyes from her chest, I looked at the hand she held out for me to shake. I stared at it for a second. Hoes didn't normally want to shake hands.

"Keyz," I told her giving her a head nod instead.

The girl quietly sat on the bench next to me. Just when I was about to get up and move away from her, her dog started barking.

Looking towards the direction the dog was barking, I saw Thugga and Lil' Thugga walking up. I exhaled in relief. My forced celibacy was beginning to get the best of me and the bitch next to me wasn't helping, moving around making her ass and titties jiggle. These hoes would do anything to get a nigga to fuck them.

"Yo, what up, my nigga," Thugga said when he approached the bench as Lil' Thugga ran off to play with Keira and Shaun.

I stood up to dap my main man off. The chick was eye fucking both of us. *How in the fuck I fuck over a good girl for bitches so forward?* The shit was seriously turning me off and was borderline disgusting. She leaned towards her handbag and fumbled around her purse for something. I stepped back from Thugga at the movement and was getting ready to pull out my gun. My guard was up and everybody was a suspect, hoes included. I chilled when she took out a pen and paper and wrote her number on it.

She grabbed her handbag, stood up, and looked up at me. "Call me sometimes."

I looked at the folded piece of paper in her hand. "I'm cool," I said nonchalantly, without taking it from her.

The chick licked her lips. I used to love when bitches did sexy shit like that, but now all I thought about was how many dicks they done sucked. I wasn't taking the bait. "I would love it if you called me."

My patience was thin at her insistence. I snapped, "Bitch, don't you see me spending time with my kids? Go 'head on with that bullshit. Ain't shit happening here. Run your lil' hot ass on somewhere." The way I was feeling about hoes, I wouldn't spit on a bitch if she was on fire.

The paper fell to the ground. "Fuck you, nigga," she said and huffed off. I didn't even pay her disrespect no mind, because I knew she was mad I didn't fall for her trap.

Thugga and I stared at her retreating back, looking at her ass. "Damn, shorty got a fat ass," Thugga said.

"There's her number. Call her." I nodded towards the ground.

Thugga shook his head. "Nah, man. I'm cool. I ain't fucking with these hoes no more. I'll look, but I ain't touching." I sat down. Thugga followed suit.

"Nikki still ain't come back?"

"Man, I think she gon' for good this time. I feel it man. I had to pick up Lil' Thugga from school. She wouldn't even see me." He leaned back and looked to the sky. I heard the distress in his voice, but I had no words of advice for him. My own shit was fucked up.

Like that old saying went, you got to sweep your own front porch, before you can swept someone else's.

We sat on the bench and watched our younguns play together. The boys hovered over Keira as she climbed the small stairs for the slide. Lil' Thugga followed her up the stairs and Shaun ran around to the end of the slide to wait for his sister to come down. My lips lifted upwards into a smile at them looking out for the female in their life. I didn't know where they got that trait from. Thugga and I could take a page from them lil' niggas. Already they were wise beyond their years.

Chapter 19

The loyalty, well held to fools, does make our faith mere folly.

-William Shakespeare

Shaunie

Ding Dong.

I stood outside of Dam's house waiting for him to answer the door. He and I had been talking on the phone almost every night since our first date two weeks ago. We decided to meet at his house for dinner and a movie for our second date. Quickly, I patted my hair, adjusted my bra, then cupped my hand over my mouth to check my breath. I removed my hand from my mouth at the sound of the door handle turning. Dam opened the door with a smile on his handsome face.

"Wow, Shaunie, you look beautiful, as always," he said.

He bent down, engulfed me in a hug after placing a kiss at the corner of my mouth. I returned the hug with one hand. When he stepped back, I raised my hand up.

"Thank you. I bought wine," I said holding up the bottle.

"Come in. Let me take that." Dam opened the door wider to allow me entry.

I admired the interior and décor of his home when I stepped in. Everything was appointed beautifully and the red and gold color scheme made everything come together. I stepped in the large foyer and looked at a picture of him, Damara, a man that looked older than Dam and an older couple I assumed were his parents.

"My older brother, Damien," he commented without further explanation.

Alright then. *Do I detect some bad feelings*? I thought. "You have a beautiful home."

"Thank you. You can place your purse on the coat rack," he said, pointing to a rack in the corner of the foyer. I put my keys in my purse before I put it on the rack. "We can go in the kitchen. Dinner is almost ready. I just have to finish the salad."

I followed him to the kitchen. The kitchen was very spacious with large windows that gave an amazing view of the yard through while letting in lots of natural lighting. The appliances were black to match the black and gold granite. He had set the table for two, with a candle burning in the middle. Dam walked to the center island where he had set the vegetables.

"I can help."

"Cool. Can you cut the cucumber? Everything you need is right there." He pointed at the cutting board and knife.

"Sure." I stood next to him as I cut the cucumber. It felt different to work side by side in the kitchen with a man. In all the years Keyz and I had been together, he never helped or offered to help in the kitchen. Not that I minded. I loved taking care of my man, but it was nice to work together on such a simple task. Dam and I finished the salad, then we bought it to the table, where Dam served me.

"A toast," Dam said as he raised his wine glass.

"And what are we toasting to?"

"A toast to us for finally spending some quality time together. I hope we have many more."

I lifted an eyebrow while I raised my glass. "Maybe," I said provocatively.

We talked about his work and my new daycare building as we ate. Sparks flew around the table as we tiptoed around our attraction. After dinner, I helped Dam clean up the kitchen. Any chance he got, he rubbed up against me. I felt the first stirrings of arousal at his touches.

Deciding to watch a movie, we headed to the living room and cuddled up on the sofa. I sat close to Dam with my feet tucked under me. He placed his arm across my shoulders and played with the strands of my hair. The sensual touch lulled me to put my head on his broad shoulder. I closed my eyes at the sexual feelings he evoked.

A gentle shaking caused me to snap my eyes open. "Wake up, sleepy head," Dam said. I lifted my head and quickly wiped my mouth in case I slobbered while I slept. "Don't worry, you don't have drool coming from your mouth." He chuckled.

I gave him a shy smile before I stood up. Lifting my arms above my head, I stretched. The action caused my breasts to thrust out and it caught Dam's rapt attention. "Sorry, I fell asleep on you. I didn't realize I was so tired."

He stood up and placed his warm hands on my hips. "No problem. I enjoyed your head on my shoulder." He pulled me close and I went willingly into his arms. His arms moved up and down my back as we stared at each other. In the intensity of his stare, I saw a lust so raw it was overwhelming, but not enough for me to step back. Hot coals of desire enflamed my body and threatened to consume me. Dam tilted his head towards me and I met him half way. Our lips connected. This kiss was more ravenous than our first kiss. He deepened the kiss and my tongue twirled against his. His hands slid to my ass cheeks, cupped the plump globes, and lifted me up. I wrapped my legs around his waist as he began walking to what I assumed was the bedroom.

We continued to tongue kiss even when he opened the door to his bedroom and placed me on the edge of the bed. He pulled my dress over my head and left me in my bra and panties. Being self-conscious because I had never been bare in front of another man besides Keyz, I placed my hand over my bra and covered my legs in an attempt to cover up.

"Don't cover up your body from me. I want to see your beautiful skin." He kissed the swell of my breast and my resistance melted like butter at the scorching touch. I leaned back with my head thrown back to allow him more access to my throat. I tugged at his shirt, but he stepped back. Insecurities flooded me. Maybe this was a mistake. I knew how to please Keyz in every way and with every touch, because he taught me how. But I didn't know what Dam liked. Will he expect me to give him oral? What position did he like? *What if I don't please him?* I thought. The questions I asked myself were making me more confused than ever. Lifting my head in confusion, I saw he wore a sexy smirk on his face. That smirk is what stopped me from fleeing from him in fear of not satisfying him. Hell, he better satisfy me.

Dam walked to the light switch and dimmed the lights. I leaned up on my elbows with my legs slightly cocked opened to watch him walk towards me. He grabbed the edge of his shirt and pulled it over his head, revealing ripped abs and caramel skin. My juices flooded my panties when I saw his hardness tenting his jeans. I saw that Dam was packing something serious when he kicked off his jeans and boxers. He was long and wide. Pre-cum oozed from the head and I licked my lips at the sight.

My legs trembled in anticipation. He stalked towards the bed, grabbed my legs to pull me to the edge of the bed, unhooked my bra and pulled my panties off. I was so horny that I didn't even care that this was just our second date. My body craved a release. I'd save my regrets over having casual sex for later. My sexual attraction for Dam was too strong to ignore.

He placed his hand on my stomach and applied pressure to force me to lay back. I laid back and closed my eyes in bliss as his mouth enclosed over a hard nipple. As he licked my breast, his hand slowly moved over my stomach, then down lower to my sweet spot. A long finger traced my clit, rubbing my flowing honey all over my pussy. His kisses followed the trail of his hand. With one swipe of his thick tongue, I arched my back. His touch was so different from Keyz, but he had serious skills. Strong arms grabbed my ankles and wrapped my legs around his neck as he went in for the kill. Dam used his tongue like a screw driver as he curled it and stuck it in and out of me. My hands found their way in his wavy hair and I pressed his head further into my body. "Aaaahhh, yes right there," I sighed in pleasure.

He licked me over and over again. "Mmmm, you taste so good. I can't get enough," he said in between tongue swipes. Then he proved that statement by going down deeper.

I started panting the closer my orgasm got. My exhausted legs fell open as they turned to jelly. He placed his hands on my inner thighs to keep them open for his access.

"I'm about to cum." I rotated my hips when he latched on to my clit. Stars exploded in front of my eyes as I came. He lapped up every drop. Exhausted from the foreplay, I sunk into the mattress. Dam gently scooped me in his arms and positioned me in the center of the bed and climbed on top of me. I wrapped my arms around his neck as he kissed me and my legs around his waist as he eased inside me.

"God this pussy so damn tight." He worked his dick inside me inch by inch. He paused for a second for me to adjust to his girth. I hadn't had sex in a minute, so I knew I felt like a vise. When my muscles loosened up, I matched his pace and began to drown in lust. My eyes closed as his strokes deepened. Keyz' image popped up behind my eyes and I stopped moving to his rhythm.

Sensing that my mind was somewhere else, he kissed me. My mind cleared of everyone and everything as I lost myself in him. My inner muscles fluttered as my climax built.

"Keep going, don't stop." I locked my ankles around his back. "Yes. Fuck me."

Increasing his pace, my head banged the headboard a few times as he pumped into me. I clenched my inner muscles when I felt him thumping inside of me. "Aaaaah shit," he moaned, then stilled as he came. When he completely emptied himself inside me, he rolled off of me and pulled me over to lay my head on his chest. We both inhaled huge gulps of air. "That was amazing."

He pulled on my hair as I used his chest as a pillow. I smiled and nodded my head to his statement. "It was the bomb.com."

"The bomb.com, huh?" He tickled my side and I giggled like a young girl. I felt so carefree in that moment. Keyz didn't cross my mind again. I wasn't concerned with the hurt. Me being here with Dam wasn't about some game of getting revenge for the shit Keyz did. It was simply me spending time and getting to know a guy who was attracted to me and I was attracted to him. Our sexual chemistry was off the charts. I wanted to be touched intimately, so

I allowed us to cross that line. There was no relationship to hold me back from exploring it. "Let's go for round two." He began to harden against my stomach.

I scooted away from him. "If you want it, you have to catch it." I batted my eyelashes playfully and put the tip of my index finger in my mouth. When I attempted to scoot away further, he caught my legs and flipped me on my stomach.

"Don't run from me. I enjoy the chase." He placed his large hand under my stomach to lift me up. I arched my back and put my head down on the pillow. In one smooth forward motion, he entered me from behind.

The remainder of the night continued the same way.

***

A light snoring in my ear and heat like a furnace woke me from a deep slumber. Dam was curled around me. I turned to look at him and smiled. If my love wasn't for someone else, I could definitely see me taking things further with him. He was smart, handsome, a gentleman, and a beast in bed. Taking his arm that was wrapped around me, I gently moved it off. I climbed out the bed and silently looked for my undergarments and dress that were scattered around the floor. I went into the bathroom and took a quick shower before I dressed.

Once I was done, I went back out into the bedroom and found Dam sitting up in bed. I walked to the bed and smiled at him. "I have to get home."

"I thought we would do breakfast. With me eating you, of course." He grabbed me and pulled me on the bed.

I squealed as I rubbed his back. "As nice as that sounds. I have to get cleaned up before I pick up my daughter."

He massaged my ass and I started to get wet. "I understand. Let me walk you out." He swung his legs over the bed, but I stopped him.

"It's okay. I'll see myself out. I know you are tired, since I wore you out."

"I wish we had time to explore your claim." He palmed my ass. I was so tempted to crawl back in his bed and let him have his way with me again. "Go ahead before I keep you here. I need to get up anyway. My brother is back home from God knows where and wants me to help him find a house."

I bent over and kissed him passionately. "I'll call you later." I walked to my car with a smile as bright as the morning sun on my face.

Chapter 20

Do not expect loyalty from one whom you have been disloyal to.

-Imam al-Hadi

Keyz
Meanwhile, across town.

Sitting in my big ass empty house, I laid on the sofa with a cold beer in my hand watching a basketball game on TV, thinking about my family. Loneliness ate away at me. When I wasn't working or chilling with my kids, I stayed at home and out of trouble. My phone chirped, letting me know I had an incoming message. Thinking it was Shaunie, I bent over to grab it. The message had my mood going from melancholy to anger real quick. Hopping off the sofa, I grabbed my toolie and car keys off the coffee table and headed to the door. Somebody was about to die. I warned her of what would happen if she fucked with another nigga.

Jontrell, Shaunie's bodyguard, reported that she had been inside of that beige nigga's house for two hours. The thought of her fucking him had me ready to commit genocide. Touching what belonged to me, I'd fuck around and kill him and his whole family.

Slamming the front door behind, I jumped in my car and started the ignition. So many emotions rioted through me, I didn't know which to give into first. I put my head on the steering wheel and took a deep breath. After the shit I put her through, I didn't want to drive over there and accuse her of shit she may not be doing. I wanted to believe she wouldn't fuck another nigga, but I could place a bet on it due to all my bullshit. I picked up my phone to call her. It rung a few times before going to voicemail.

"I need you to call me asap." I left a voicemail, hung up, and walked back to the house. When I got inside, I immediately poured myself a glass of Patron. I took the glass of Patron and the bottle to the bedroom with me and changed into a pair of sweats. After grabbing a rolled blunt, I walked outside to the patio that's attached to our bedroom. I sat in the chair and tossed back, feeling miserable as fuck, because Shaunie barely talks to me and now she was entertaining another nigga.

Placing the bottle of alcohol on the table, I checked my phone to see if I had a missed call or message from her. I knew I didn't, because it didn't ring or chirp, but waiting was killing me. I called her again.

"Bae, call me. We need to talk about Keira. Call me back." Fuck it, I wasn't above using my baby girl to get at her mama. I sent her a text message, too. I leaned back in the chair and tossed back another glass. It was close to 10 pm and the stars in the sky twinkled. The air and sky seemed so peaceful and tranquil, but I was anything but. *Will she fuck him?* I asked myself. *Will I take her back if she does?* Thoughts of her fucking and being happy with someone other than me consumed be and burned like a wildfire. My hand clenched around the glass before I threw it and it shattered on impact. I stared at the numerous shards for a second. The pieces of the shattered glass seemed to go everywhere, like my thoughts and my heart.

"Fuck!"

My head fell back against the chair and I rubbed my hands down my face. I could go over there and act a fucking fool, but I would risk the chance of pushing her away further. But I felt like a bitch sitting here while she was over by some nigga. When I removed my hands, the bottle of alcohol caught my attention. Picking it up, I drunk straight from the bottle like the answers to the universe was inside it. I proceeded to drink the bottle and get shit-faced drunk as I sent Shaunie several messages and called numerous times, but all had gone unanswered. I was hoping that my calls and messages would deter her from doing anything if I my calls kept interrupting them.

Startled awake at the ringing of the phone, which was in my lap, I quickly grabbed it, hoping it was Shaunie. I had a headache and my vision was slightly blurred. It was almost sunrise and I slept in a chair on the patio. The number on the screen dashed any hope I had that my girl was calling.

"Yo, what's up?" I asked Jontrell.

"She just now leaving from ole dude's house." The news that she practically spent the night hurt a nigga bad. Here I was sulking and shit behind her and she out enjoying life.

"Make sure she gets home safely," I said, hanging up. I went inside, handled my hygiene, put on a shirt and some shoes and left the house. As I made my way to Shaunie's house, I thought about what I would say to her, because I had no clue. When I made it to her house, she still hadn't arrived yet, so I parked on the street, got out my car and sat on the doorstep and waited for her.

After fifteen minutes of waiting, she pulled into the driveway. With her heels in her hand, she walked up to the door and saw me sitting on the doorstep. Her faced showed shocked to see me waiting outside for her.

"What are you doing here, Keyon?" Her cheeks flamed when she saw me staring intently at her.

I looked her up and down. Her hair and clothes were disheveled. Seeing her appearance let me know what she had obviously been up to and it made me feel angry and hurt, but not enough to do her harm. I stood up and towered over her.

"Where you been?" I asked, getting to the point. I knew where she was, but I wanted to see if see would admit it. I schooled my face into a mask of indifference, but let my concern bleed out in my voice. After the incident at the club, I didn't want Shaunie to be skittish around me. *Stay calm. Keep cool.*

"Where I been is none of your business." She walked around me, unlocked and opened the door. When she attempted to go inside, I grabbed her bicep to stop her.

"Answer the fucking question." She jerked her arm from me and stepped inside the house, leaving the door half-way open.

She gave my hand that grabbed her arm the side eye. "Get your fucking hand off me, before you lose that bitch." Shaunie never used to talk so jazzy, but it turned me on to hear her talk shit. Putting her hand on her hip, she said, "I was at my friend Dam's house."

Even tho' I knew where she was, it still hurt to hear her admit it. I clenched my jaw and looked away before I turned back to face her and asked, "Did you fuck him?" My hearted pounded as I awaited her answer.

Shaunie took so long to respond, I didn't think she would answer me, In the doorway, she stood up taller, narrowed her eyes, and folded her arms across her chest.

"What's it to you if I did? You the pussy patrol now? How about you watch your dirty dick and I'll watch my kitty cat."

I grabbed hold of her face in one hand and gave it a little squeeze. "Don't make me put my hands on yo ass." I wasn't really going to hit her, but I needed her to answer me. Not knowing was fucking up my head.

"Try it, motherfucker. We gon' be out here fighting like cats and dogs until the sun come up." Her face darkened and a dangerous glint banked her hazel eyes. Her grip on her heels tightened as she dared me to follow through on my threat. The calmness in her voice gave me pause. Her soft tone belied her stance. If a made a wrong move towards her, I knew she would attack me. I had a flashback of Thugga's face when Nikki beat him with her heel. I wasn't trying to lose an eye, so I let her go.

"Did you fuck him?" I asked as I took a step back.

She grabbed the door and closed it a little bit. "Let's just say my catch back game is strong as fuck," she said with an evil smirk on her face. Her words hit me like a sledge hammer, as it obliterated what hope I had been holding on to that she didn't fuck another nigga. I took a step towards her and she tried to close the door in my face, but I put my foot in the crack. She leaned all her weight on the door and I pushed it with my shoulder, causing her to stumble back. "Get the fuck out my house," she whispered harshly.

The door slammed against the wall from the force, leaving an imprint of the knob in the wall. I wasn't worried about the noise rousing anyone. Keira was at my mama's house and Lil' Thugga was with his daddy. Nikki was in the house, but I wasn't concerned about her. When I stepped inside the house, she grabbed the vase off the table and threw it at me. I ducked and it shattered against the wall behind me. The shards bounced and cut the back of my arms. She ran up the stairs, but I was right on her heels.

"Don't run. Talk that shit now," I said as I grabbed one of her ankles as she ran up the stairs. She only made it up five stairs.

She used her hands to catch her fall and her other leg to kick at me. "Let me the fuck go, with your hoe ass!" Her heel connected with my eye and I saw stars. My shit felt like it started swelling.

"Uugh fuck!" I yelled without letting go. She continued to kick and I pulled her down the stairs by her leg. I wasn't worried that she would get hurt, because the stairs were carpeted and I pulled her slowly. When I pulled her all the way down, I grabbed her hair and forced her to turn around as I laid on top of her on the floor.

"You better be lucky you didn't hurt me or I would stab your stupid ass." She begin to slap me upside my head. Her lil' slaps packed some power.

Grabbing her wrists in one hand, I pent them above her head. She turned her head and bit the side of my face.

"Fuck! Let my face go." I didn't move, because I was worried she would take a chunk of my skin with her.

"Let my fucking wrists go."

"You first."

She gave me the do I look stupid look. So, I let go first, then she released my face. Immediately, I grabbed hold of her wrists again and burrowed my head in the crook of her neck, so she couldn't bite me again. I pressed my hardness between the conjunct of her thighs, eliciting a moan from her.

"You want to be fucked, huh? Well, Imma fuck you." My hand traveled to her crotch and I ripped her panties off. I moved my sweat pants down and pulled my dick out.

She wiggled underneath me to get away. I pressed more of my weight on her to make her keep still.

174

"Stop, Keyz," she said in a throaty, breathless voice, while rolling her wetness again me. I knew she wanted me to fuck her, because I went from Keyon to Keyz. "Don't stop," she said when my tip bumped her entrance.

Without releasing her wrists, I slid inside her. My eyes rolled to the back of my head at the warmth of her sheath. It felt like heaven on earth being inside of her after so long. No other woman could make me feel like this during sex. "Mmmmh, shit," I moaned and let her hands go. I stroked her hard and deep.

Her nails raked down my back and I enjoyed the sting. "Oooohhh, Keyz, yes baby. Like that." She used her inner muscles to grip me and she threw it back. "God, I miss this dick."

I pulled out to the tip and rammed into her again. "Fuck. You feel so good." Using my hand, I hiked her leg up and impaled her to the hilt.

"Aaaah!" Her cream coated me as she released her orgasm. I slipped my tongue in her mouth and silenced her scream.

I felt my nut building, so I started pounding her like a jackhammer. "Damn, bae. Aaaaaahhhh," I moaned as I released my seed inside her. I laid my head in the crook of her neck and thought about everything we had been through. Then I thought about my reason for coming here. My eyes closed as the pain overtook my sexual release.

Shaunie stroked my back, ignorant of my inner turmoil.

"Baby, that was so good." She placed a kissed to my jaw before running her hand through my dreads. "I missed you."

I wanted to tell her how much I missed her, but my pain and anger at her fucking someone else started to take a hold of me.

"Why?" I croaked out.

Her hands stilled at my question. "Why what, Keyz?"

"You fucked him?'

Tension radiated from her body. "It wasn't planned. It just happened. I'm not going to lie though. I was physically attracted to him."

My hands tangled in her hair and I applied slight pressure. I turned my mouth to her ear. "I fucked up, but I fucking love you girl," I whispered to her as a tear slipped from my eyes.

"I love you, too. I'm willing to try again if you are."

Releasing her hair, I used my hand to push myself off of her. Averting my eyes from her. "I don't know if I can. I don't think I could let go of the fact you fucked someone else." I fixed my clothes and headed to the door.

"So, what's good for you, ain't good for me? You can fuck a bunch of bitches, plus have a baby on my ass and I'm supposed to just accept it with no problem. But I slept with someone else, while we were separated, I might add, and you can't deal. You know what? Get your selfish ass out my motherfucking house and don't come around this bitch unless it's about our daughter."

A veil came down over my features to skillfully construct a wall around my emotions.

"Get rid of that nigga before you force me to kill him." I loved my girl so much. She was mine and I was possessive over what and who I considered mine. For Shaunie, my *love knows no boundaries.*

"Do you hear me, Keyon? I mean it on my baby's grave! Keep your black ass away from me." She picked up her heel and threw it at me.

The heel hit me in my back, but I didn't turn around. I knew everything she said was true and I was selfish to not take her back after she slept with someone else, considering I cheated on her plenty of times and got another bitch pregnant. But the way my heart and trigger finger was set up, I would have to kill the dude for fucking her and I knew she wasn't going to be cool with someone losing their life because she fucked them. I couldn't have no nigga walking around knowing he knew how my pussy felt. Keeping my mouth closed, I walked out of her house and maybe her heart.

Chapter 21

What makes a woman beautiful is her loyalty to and her friendships with other women, and her honesty with men.

-*Vanessa Marcil*

Shaunie

It had been a week since the incident at my house with Keyz. I didn't know how to feel about him walking out on me after we made love on the floor and then he told me he didn't think we could get back together after I slept with Dam. I couldn't help but feel used by him. He came and fucked me like I didn't matter, then left. Again, he showed no regards for my feelings. My heart ached at the thought of not being with him, but Dam was slowly filling that void with companionship. It was so nice to talk and be around him with no expectations.

Keyz hadn't called or been by to check on Keira or me. I knew he was in his feelings about the Dam situation, but it was what it was. If he couldn't accept what I did, then we didn't need to be together. I had to keep myself together for me and my daughter, so here I was, along with Nikki, on a Sunday, organizing the furniture around in my daycare. Kid's Kingdom Learning Academy was scheduled to open tomorrow. The demands of getting my center opened served as a distraction from my relationship problems.

"I put the kid's registration papers in the file cabinet in alphabetical order," Nikki said.

I rearranged the toys on the shelf for the umpteenth time, before I stepped back to make sure everything was in place.

"Did you make sure each folder had a copy of the kid's shot records?"

She smacked her teeth. "Yes, boss lady. I made folders for each child. Each folder has registration papers and copy of shot records, just like you said, ten times."

Walking back to the toy shelf, I picked up a rubber toy and threw it at her. "Stop mocking me, heifer."

We burst out laughing at our playful banter with each other.

"Everything looks nice and in place. We are all set for tomorrow. Are you excited?"

Exhaling loudly, I turned to her. "I am excited about this new venture. This daycare center is what I always wanted. I'm trying not to let my excitement get overshadowed with thoughts of my relationship problems."

"Well, focus on making this place successful. Your problems with Keyz need to take a back seat while you pursue your dreams."

I thought about what she said. When Keyz was coming up in the streets, many days and nights I took a back seat until he got settled. I never doubted I was his girl, but he used to run the streets all night, until he was somewhat satisfied with his success.

"You are absolutely correct. My dream is becoming my reality and I need to give it my all."

As we talked, we walked to the front of the building where the office was located. "I'm glad I get to work with you. I need to become more financially independent since I left Thugga. I mean I have a diploma, but no work skills. How did I let myself come to this?"

"The same way I let myself come to this. We got so wrapped up in the men we loved, somewhere along the way, we loved them more than ourselves."

"Well, it's time for me to start worrying about me first. I let that shit with Thugga and the cheating go for too long. I should have left when I first found out."

I understood where she was coming from. I, too, needed to take some responsibility for my situation with Keyz. My love was so blind for him. In spite of me never being in a relationship before or having dealt with a man, how could I not have known something? Like those Jordan's in the trunk of his car he claimed were for Lil' Corey. Now that I think on it, they weren't his size, plus he already had that pair. I shook my head at my own ignorance. *Where was my good sense?* I asked myself.

"I hear ya, sista. But it's a new me now. I am not going to sit around and be little miss stupid anymore either."

"I hear you, boo. Hurry up and let's go before you are late for your lunch date with Dam." Dam and I tried to spend time whenever our schedules allowed. He had been busy helping his brother get settled. His older brother, Damien, had just moved back home.

I checked my watch and saw I had forty-five minutes to meet up with him. We grabbed our purses and headed out the door. Nikki walked towards her car as I locked up the center. I looked up at the sign above the door and smiled. Many things happened recently in my life, but some where things to make me smile. Turning, I walked to my car and Nikki rolled down the window to her car when I walked by.

"Let me know if you need anything for tomorrow and I could run and get it."

"Thanks, babe."

"Anything for you," she said.

"And everything for you," I replied as I got in my car and pulled off.

***

We laid in bed panting, trying to catch our breath from our sexathon.

"I made that ass tap out." Dam pulled me to him and placed a soft kiss to my lips.

"I been at work all day moving furniture. I'm tired." I slapped his chest playfully as I sat up.

"I told you I would have come and done that if you had allowed me to. I want to spend every minute I can with you."

"I know, but I didn't want to take you away from helping your brother."

"Damien could have handled his business himself. I don't have to drop everything in my life since the prodigal son has returned." I heard some resentment in his voice, so I asked him some questions.

"What's the deal with your brother? You speak his name like you don't like him."

He sighed. "It's not that I don't like him. We are a few years apart, but never clicked. Our personalities are just different. He is bad news and always in some trouble, so my parents catered to him more than me and Damara. I'm glad he is trying to get his life together." I pulled me closer. "Enough about him, let's talk about us. I really enjoy being with you. I know we haven't been seeing each other long, but I want to make this official."

As tempting as it sounded, I couldn't trust it not to be a game. If my time with Keyz didn't teach me anything else, it taught me that a man would say anything to get a woman, but do only half of what's required to keep her. I refuse to be any man's half-time, down-time, spare-time, or some-time. It's all or nothing with me and for me. So I would not waste my time. Besides, I didn't think I would ever be able to fully commit to anyone after what I have had to deal with. In spite of my hurt, my heart still beat for Keyz.

"Dam, I always have an amazing time with you and I truly enjoy our conversations. But, I just got out of a long-term relationship and to be honest, I still love him and probably always will. I'm not even sure if I am completely done with him."

His face tightened with something akin to disappointment.

"I am not going to lie and say I am not a little upset. I'm definitely feeling you and would love nothing more than to explore where this could go. But, I'm glad you are being honest before feelings get too involved." He kissed me again. The kiss felt like a good-bye and I was okay with that. My emotions were all over the place. I didn't know what I wanted. Dam was wanted I needed at the time. I needed someone to talk to and a chance to just live. There was no expectations between us and I enjoyed that. My attraction to him helped to distract me from my problems and feelings that I had been going through with Keyz. I had to step back from him and walk away, because I didn't want to be with someone and use them as a rebound when I had feelings for someone else.

"Thank you for being honest with me."

"Thank you for understanding." I touched his face and stared in his eyes. Dam was everything I wanted in a man, at least what he showed me. Getting out of the bed, I put my clothes on and grabbed my heels off the floor. I walked to the door and left the house without looking back.

Chapter 22

Loyalty cannot be blueprinted. It cannot be produced on an assembly line. In fact, it cannot be manufactured at all, for its origin is the human heart, the center of self-respect and human dignity. It is a force which leaps into being only when conditions are exactly right for it, and it is a force very sensitive to betrayal.

-Maurice Franks

Keyz

An arm landing on my chest caused me to jolt awake. I woke up disoriented from a hangover and popping pills. Looking to the left of me, two bitches were curled up together, naked. To my right were two more bitches positioned the same way. I felt dirty with these freak bitches laying in bed with me. Disgusted with myself, I shook my head. I had been doing good and stayed faithful to my girl for months. Hell, I couldn't even stay hard watching porn.

Leaning back with my eyes closed, last night's events played out. I didn't remember much, but drinking and popping them trams. Them Tramadols be having at nigga fucked up. I needed something to numb my pain, because every time I closed my eyes, thoughts of Shaunie and the light-skinned nigga fucking, burned my eyes. Thugga and my bodyguard half carried me to the hotel room with the hoes trailing behind. I groaned out loud. *How in the fuck I let myself get this fucked up?* This was how niggas got caught slipping. *I got too much shit going on to be fucking up like this.*

The ordeal with Shaunie had me fucked up. I killed two of my workers for simple shit that could have warranted an ass beating. Instead, I used my 9mm and shot them. One worker was talking to a bitch instead of selling to a fiend and the other worker had a smart retort when I told him something. I didn't even remember what he said, because I just black out. Not trusting myself to handle my homicidal rampage, I had turned into a hermit the past week, so I isolated myself to get my feelings in check. It took everything in me to not kill the nigga she had been with. The only thing that stopped me was knowing she would never forgive me and my sins towards her were already stacked high. I had acknowledged that I was the reason she ran to another nigga in the first place. And here I was back to the same shit.

I looked at the arms draped over my chest with disgust. Scooting to the edge of the bed, I got out and grabbed my phone to dial Rayne.

"Yo, my nigga. You good?" he asked me.

"Yeah, man, I'm cool. Did that package at the warehouse come around yet?" I asked him in code, speaking of the nigga from the shootout a few weeks back. The nigga was on his death bed, but the doctor stabilized his ass. I had a hard-on for this nigga and needed answers like yesterday.

"I was just about to call you. Dude been up since last night, but when I hit you up, you was fucked up."

"It's all good. It ain't like the nigga going anywhere." I pinched the bridge of my nose as a headache began.

"You want me to swing by and scoop you up?" Rayne asked me.

"Yeah, man." I told him where I was. "Hey, I need a favor. Pick up some pills at the pharmacy for me." When he asked what kind, I told him and he laughed.

When I got off the phone, I headed to the bathroom. Morning erection in hand, I released my bladder. I almost sighed with relief when it didn't burn. I walked to the door, looked out and saw my bodyguard posted up at the door. I gave him a head nod. Dude definitely deserved a bonus for pulling an all-nighter.

"Yo, Rayne is on his way up. Let him in, but don't let any of these bitches leave."

"Got it, boss."

I went back to the bathroom and jumped in the shower to wash. I was dead tired and had a hangover, so I turned the water on hot to help wake myself up. The soap wasn't as good as mine at home and the quick shower wasn't much, but it would do until I got home. The scent from the hoes washed down the drain, so did my anger and pain at Shaunie. It was my fault that we're in the place we were in. I missed her so much, but when she opened up to me, I couldn't swallow my pride. She didn't cheat on me like I cheated on her. She repeatedly told me we weren't together, but I didn't want to hear it. In my eyes, she will always be mine.

It was time for me to get my girl back. I was tired of spending the night alone and I knew she was missing me, too. The day at her crib she told me she missed me and her eyes pleaded with me for us to try to work past our problems. Imma have to tell her about this cluster fuck I let myself get in with this hoes in the hotel room with me. No more secrets and lies.

Hopping out the shower, I dried off and slipped back on the clothes from the previous night. As I headed out the bathroom, a knock sounded at the door. I grabbed my 9mm off the nightstand and looked through the peephole to discover Rayne with a pharmacy bag. The knocking must have woke up the girls, because they got out of bed and started putting on their clothes.

Lowering my gun, I opened the door. "What up, man?" I man hugged him. "I appreciate you picking that up for me," I said nodding to the bag.

"Dawg, I got you." He passed me the bag and sat in a chair.

I turned to the women who were fully dressed, if you could call all that exposed skin that, lounging on the bed. *Fuck.* I could kick myself for this shit.

"It time for y'all to bounce," I said getting straight to the point. "Before y'all go, y'all need to take these." I handed each of them a plan B contraception pill and a bottle of water.

One girl scrunched up her nose. "Is this the morning after pill?"

"Yeah, ma. Ain't nobody claiming no babies if I slipped up."

She shrugged her shoulder, took the pill, and drunk some water. Two of the other girls followed suit without question.

The last remaining girl looked affronted. "Slipped up? Nigga, you couldn't even get it up."

I took no offense at her words, because my knees weakened at the knowledge that I didn't fuck any of them.

"Good. Because y'all are poor ass substitutes for who I wanted anyway." I wasn't sober when we arrived at the hotel and any action that would have taken place would have been against what I wanted. "Then, bitch, you shouldn't have no problem taking it anyway." I found my voice. Even though they stated that nothing happened, I wasn't taking no chances. I also had to schedule an appointment with my doctor.

She glared at me before taking the pill and drinking some water. Once she was done she stomped to the door.

"Rayne. Check that hoes mouth and make sure she swallowed." When the girl started to protest, I cut her off. "Pry her mouth open if you have to."

He got up and did as I asked him. He mumbled something to the girl that killed any protest that came to her lips.

I walked over to the other girls, who remained silent at the exchange between me and the fourth girl. I grabbed my wallet from my back pocket, pulled out some bills, and handed each girl five hundred dollars. "Y'all take a cab home."

They grabbed the money, but one girl spoke as she did. "You know, nothing happened. You talked about somebody named Shaunie all night."

I nodded my head at her and left the room.

**

I called up my inner circle and sergeants to meet at the warehouse as I drove there. The shooter was up and I was going to torture information out of him. My crew needed to be reminded of how I got down and I wanted to watch for reactions to see if they would give themselves away. My safety wasn't an issue, because everyone had to lock their weapons up, but me. If one of them was talking, they needed to see how I was going to handle them. With no remorse.

Everyone was present and waiting in the basement when I made it there. Rayne and Thugga was posted next to the nigga who shot at us. The nigga looked weak and sunken laying on a pallet in the corner with his eyes closed and an IV in his vein. That shit wasn't going to deter me. I walked to the area where he was, crouched down, and yanked the IV from his arm.

"Wake up, nigga. You ain't on no fucking vacation." His eyes popped open at the sound of my voice and the pain in his arm caused. "Now, I'm only going to ask this nicely once before shit gets ugly. Who the fuck you working for and where can I find them niggas?" I asked him quietly. I used caution, because I didn't want anyone to hear any info he had to offer. The only thing I wanted them to hear were his screams.

The nigga looked me in the eye with defiance. "I ain't saying shit, so kill me now, nigga, 'cause you gon' do it anyway," he said in a weak, tired voice. He had balls, I had to give him that, but those balls was gon' be removed, painfully, if he didn't cooperate.

"Smart man. You ain't leaving here alive, that's true. However, your last remaining minutes on earth can go two ways. One, you tell me what I need and I just shoot you. Two, I painfully force you to tell me. Trust me when I say, by the time I'm done working you over, you gon' talk."

He seemed to contemplate the offer for a second. Then he spit at my feet. I was glad he spat at my feet and not my face, because there was no way in hell I would be able to stop myself from killing him on the spot at the sign of disrespect. I cocked my fist back and slammed it down on his abdomen on his bullet wound.

"Uuuuuurrrrrrgggggg," he grunted in pain, gasping for breath and holding his stomach.

I stood up and took a step back. "Put his ass in the chair," I told Thugga and Rayne. They picked him up and strapped his hands and legs to the chair. Not saying a word to my crew, I walked over to the shelves with the tools and thought of what I wanted to do first. Grabbing the branding iron and blow torch, I threw the iron on the concrete floor and used the blow torch to heat the end. Not worried that the heat would burn my skin, due to my protective leather gloves, I picked the now blazing hot branding iron up and walked towards the chair.

He started fighting against his restraints, but didn't beg. The chair lifted off the floor he fought so hard.

"Wait," he said when I was two feet from him.

Since I went through the trouble of heating the branding iron, it was only fair that I used it, so I ignored him.

"Hold his head back," I instructed Thugga.

"Man, watch that fucking iron. I ain't tryna get burned in this bitch," Thugga said as he grabbed the nigga's head.

I stepped forward and pressed the branding iron to his right eye.

"Aaaaaaaauuuuuugggghhhhh!" he screeched. Bucking in the chair as his skin sizzled like bacon in a frying pan. The smell of burning flesh permeated the basement that was too small to accommodate all the men in the room and the torture. I heard someone gag and it bought a smirk to my lips.

"Imma talk. Stop."

"So, you want to talk now? Well, now I want to play." I burned his other eye and he slumped in his chair, all the fight leaving him and he passed out from the pain. I gave him a minute to recover while I addressed my men. "Y'all niggas remember this shit. When you try to fuck me around, I'm going to fuck you harder and with no Vaseline. Imma kill you, then go after your entire bloodline to prove my point. Don't test me." I turned back to my plaything and woke him up with a smelling salt. The ammonia gas worked instantly. "Now, let the real fun begin."

After twenty minutes of working him over using different tools, with my crew standing by looking nervous and nauseous, I asked him again who he was working for and where I could find them. He didn't have a name for the head nigga in charge or his second in command, because he never met them, but he did have a location of a house in Slidell that he whispered in a voice that didn't allow anyone, but me, to hear. Using discretion so the other members of my crew didn't learn this new info, Rayne pulled up the location on Satellite Google Earth. Once the location was confirmed from the description the nigga gave, it was time to end my session. I shot him twice in the head and turned to Thugga.

"Cut him up and feed him to the gators." I looked at every nigga in the room. Some made eye contact with a flinch and some looked away with a fidget. Good. I wanted them niggas to fear me.

"Rayne, give them their guns from the storage lockers. Y'all are dismissed." They ran out the basement like the hounds of hell were behind them, leaving me and my inner crew behind.

"Yo, did he offer any info?" Killer asked.

I side-eyed that nigga. The suspicion that was cast on my inner crew members from the hit on my delivery was never far from my mind. My interactions with Killer, Qwan, and the rest on my crew were kept to a minimum. Hell, even Thugga and Rayne seemed suspect at moments. So the question Killer asked seemed suspicious as fuck at a time like this.

"Is there any particular reason why you want to know?" I couldn't stop the accusatory tone that dripped with my words.

"Damn, nigga, don't bite my head off. I'm just asking," he said, holding his hands up. I was trying to keep my cool so them niggas didn't know I knew someone on the team was a traitor, but it was getting harder every day to not knock off both Killer and Qwan.

"Alejandro has some family business to take care of in Colombia. Because business is business, it don't stop for personal shit, and we both gon' lose money, he is sending a couple of keys to hold us, since he is going to be away for the re-up date." My connect frequently traveled from the US to Colombia, since his father was the head of the Medillin Cartel.

"That's what's up. What you need us to do?" Qwan asked. It was hard to reconcile he would betray the team. He was always ready to go hard.

"Thugga is going to meet up with Alejandro's people and pick up the package. I don't want to bring it to the drop-off location to be distributed yet, since we are still fresh with what we just got. So, like last time when we got early product, when he comes through on Thursday, I want you to drop it off at the house where we just had our monthly meeting," I said looking at Thugga.

"Do you want me to arrange a team to sit on the spot?" Rayne asked.

I thought about it for a second, but I already had my answer. "Nah, it's good. The place is secure. Every nigga need to be out grinding, 'cause numbers been slipping, ya feel me."

"For real, For real," Thugga responded.

Like countless meetings before, I asked them if they had anything to add to the plan and we all agreed it was rock solid. My mind was in overdrive thinking of who all was involved. It was time for the snake nigga to show his face.

Chapter 23

I belong to the people I love, and they belong to me – they, and the love and loyalty I give them, form my identity far more than any word or group ever could.

-Veronica Roth

Shaunie

Putting my hair in a messy bun after my shower, I bounded down the stairs to grab my wine before I relaxed in bed for the night. Keira was with her dad, so I allowed myself to drink a few glasses of wine and chill. Seeing that nothing good was on TV after I channel surfed for fifteen minutes, I put on my K. Michelle's CD, *Anybody Wanna Buy a Heart,* and let the music play. The vibration of my phone on the nightstand broke my trance. I grabbed it, swiped the screen, and read the message. My brows furrowed in confusion.

Getting out of bed quickly, I went back downstairs to open the door.

"What happened?" I asked Keyz as I stepped back and allowed him to enter with a crying Keira in his arms.

"She kept crying for you. I tried calling you, but it went to voicemail." He bounced Keira up and down in an attempt to get her to quiet down. Despite everything, I loved how he loves our daughter. He was so patient and gentle with her.

"I was in the shower." I reached out to grab my baby. "Come to…"

Keira pulled her arm from me. "No. I want daddy." She wrapped her arms around her daddy and squeezed tighter.

I looked at Keyz with my head tilted sideways. For him to claim she cried for me, but refused to come to me was strange, but I brushed it off.

"Since she doesn't want to come to me, can you just bathe her and tuck her in bed until she falls asleep?"

"You know you don't even have to ask." He headed to the stairs. "Which door?"

"Second to the left," I said as I followed him up the stairs, but continued to my bedroom. Keyz and I fit together like pieces of a puzzle. Even going through all of the madness, there was a level of comfortability between us that only years together could create.

We were always so in tuned with each other's feelings and thoughts.

Once inside, I sat up in bed with my back against the pillows and thought about how clingy Keira had been with her dad. It broke my heart that the separation caused anxiety for my baby. She was used to a two parent home. Her routine was changed overnight several months back and she hadn't adjusted yet. Hell, I hadn't adjusted to living separately from the man my heart yearned for. K. Michelle's *Hard To Do* played over the speakers, I got up and put it on repeat. Closing my eyes, I listened to the song.

I've been thinking 'bout ya
Are you thinking 'bout me?
I know I went crazy
But you were wrong
I apologize, I'll let it go tonight
Forgive me and I'll forgive you

The sound of the door creaking open caused me to open my eyes. His eyes connected with mine. We stared intently at each other, we both didn't want to be the first to break contact. I tracked his movements as he walked towards my bed and sat on the edge.

Lifting my feet onto his lap, he began to massage them. *Oooohhh,* my inner self moaned. *God, how I miss the simple ways he took care of me.*

Music playing in the background, now that our focus was on each other, the time of reckoning had come. This is where it all comes to a head. I knew he wanted to sit down and talk, so did I. "Let's talk," we said simultaneously. We shared a small smile at our words, because we used to do it all the time.

I tilted my head, allowing him to go first.

"You first." I grabbed my wine glass and gulped the contents down in one swallow. Since my accidental overdose, I had been mindful of my alcohol consumption, but I needed something to calm my nerves, because I knew this was going to be explosive.

"I want to say that I love you and I'm sorry for everything I put you through. I'm not going to sit here and make any excuses to justify my transgressions. I acknowledge that I was wrong. I want my family back. I need y'all," he said sincerely. His eyes never moved away from mind.

I stared at him for a minute. My thoughts and words were all over the place and I didn't know where to start first.

"Tell me what you wanted when you were out there doing you, because I know for damn sure I wasn't lacking in any area."

During our separation, I racked my mind searching every area of my life and questioning myself to see how and where I had been slipping in my duties to him as a helpmate, to cause him to step out on me, but I kept drawing blanks. Not one single instance came to mind.

He was silent as he thought of his actions and chose his words correctly.

"You didn't lack at all. I was the one lacking. I didn't think about how my actions would hurt you. I thought about my own feelings and ego." He took a deep breath before he continued. "We were young when we settled down. You were seventeen and I was just turning twenty. I don't think I was truly ready to settle with one woman at the time. You were everything I wanted, even thought I wasn't looking. I couldn't chance letting you go and another man stepping up to snatch you up."

His words struck a nerve and I jumped up out the bed and got in his face.

"You knew I had never been with anyone, in a relationship or otherwise. You took fucking advantage of me and my inexperience," I said, pointing my index finger in his face. "If you wasn't ready to settle the fuck down, then you shouldn't have pursued me and convinced me otherwise." I mushed his head away before I turn and stepped away from the bed. My chest was heaving up and down as I got heated. "You apologize for your cheating like that's supposed to fix it."

"Baby, I'm not apologizing for just cheating. I'm apologizing for betraying your trust, destroying our relationship, and for embarrassing you." He held his hands out in a pleading gesture. Pleading with me for his family back.

I didn't pay his pleading any mind, because I was on one and went in on him.

"How could you do this to me?" I asked, pointing to and stabbing my chest to emphasis the important role I played in his life the past seven years. I turned away for a second to get my composure. I'd be damned if I cried behind him again.

"Bae, hear me out."

"No. Shut up and you listen." I moved to the middle of the room, because I didn't trust myself not to hit him. "I was down for you when no one was. Me! I broke my fucking back working to help ya ass come up. When you was out fucking around, I was home building a life and family for us. I loss two of my babies behind your ass."

Our talking turned into screaming. We weren't listening to each other. Whenever he talked, I yelled over him. In my anger, I pounded a fist in my hand at every word I spoke. The fussing and cussing with on for about an hour.

After all the yelling, my voice was hoarse and Keyz hung his head down in shame. I didn't know if this talk fixed anything or helped.

"I have no faith in you," I whispered as I looked away with my arms hugging myself. Forgiveness wasn't even the issue at this point. The hardest part of all of this was trying to figure out how to get back to what we had.

He got off the bed and walked towards me and pulled me in his embrace. I allowed it, because I needed the comfort.

"Shaunie," he said, lifting my face to his. "Don't have faith in who I was. My decisions made me feel like that nigga in the streets. To know I had my wifey at home, but could still pull bitches and do dumb shit." His thumb moved back and forth, caressing my cheek. "But you, you make me feel like a man. With you, I am a man. You let me be the provider and protector for you and our child. You allowed me to do things for you, even when you don't really need me." Memories of all the good times we had together played out before me. All the little things he did to make me happy flashed in my mind. I remembered all the back and foot rubs. The moment when I gave birth to our daughter and him kissing me and telling me how proud and happy he was. He held me in his strong arms when my dad died. Movie nights at home. Breakfast in bed. Small trinkets as tokens of love. I had been so focused on what he did wrong, I forgot about everything he did right.

We stared in each other's eyes, searching for the love that bonded us together. Slowly, his head dipped towards mine and his lips hovered before mine, but he didn't kiss me. He allowed me to make that decision. I read in his eyes that if I kissed him, I would seal our relationship back together and we would try to move forward. If I didn't kiss him, he would try to let me live my life without him. So many choices in our relationship had been taken away from me, intentionally or otherwise. I loved him more for giving me this choice.

Raising on my tiptoes, I softly pressed my lips to his. He wrapped his arms around my waist and I slid my hands to his shoulders, pulling each other closer. His tongue came out and swiped across my lips for an invitation to access the warm crevice of my mouth. Parting my lips on a sigh, I let him inside. There wasn't a part of my mouth that his tongue didn't touch.

Our tongues twirled when he deepened the kiss. Keyz placed his hands on the back of my head and began walking me backwards, towards the bed. His lips were clamped to mine with a sense of urgency. Before my back could even hit the mattress, he placed a hand on either side of me. His manhood pressed against my stomach and my heart started beating faster.

"You're mine." He sounded so fucking possessive, I creamed my panties.

With impatient hands, we took off each other's clothes. Despite being overheated with passion, the chilled air that greeted my bare flesh caused goosebumps. My name on his chest, across his heart, caught my eyes and I fought tears. I leaned forward and kissed the brand that labeled him as mine. Laying my head on the mattress, I closed my eyes as the teardrops escaped against my restrain. He placed a light kiss on both eyelids that caused my eyes to flutter. Then, he lowered his mouth to my neck and skillfully, like the master of my body, lit a fire that burned hot when his lips caressed my sensitive spot. Kisses from my neck to my shoulders had me feigning to feel him inside me.

"Please," I begged. I grabbed his hard length and gave it a few strokes. "I want you inside of me."

"Baby, I love you," he said as he moved his hips and placed himself at my entrance. The feel of the tip of his erection had me clenching in anticipation. "Imma love you forever." He kissed me hard and deep. Finally, he entered me and I rocked my hips to his rhythm, a pattern we were used to. Everything faded. It was just me and Keyz, with K. Michelle's *Hard To Do*, playing in the background.

Oh, baby cause...
Missing you is way too hard to do
I'd rather be fucking you
Do you mind if I give you love
'Cause I just wanna give you love
Won't you tell me if I'm doing too much
Missing you is way too hard to do

Chapter 24

A person is born with feelings of envy and hate. If he gives way to them, they will lead him to violence and crime, and any sense of loyalty and good faith will be abandoned.

-Xun Zi

Keyz

A glorious smell woke me from my slumber. I looked around in confusion before a smile split my lips. With my head on the pillow, I closed my eyes and thought about last night. Making love to my girl brought me so much peace, I got a full night's rest for the first time in months. Nothing felt better than Shaunie's soft skin infused with vanilla. I hopped out of bed and made my way to the kitchen. My bae was at the stove cooking. Walking up behind her, I wrapped my arms around her waist.

"Good morning," I said as I placed a kiss to her neck and pressed my morning erection into her back.

She turned around and hesitantly placed her arms on my shoulders. Her hesitation caused me a moment of panic. I thought she was going to change her mind about us being back together.

"Good morning," she said in a quiet voice.

The silence that filled the kitchen was an awkward one, like two people who had a one-night stand and the morning after, they didn't know what to say to each other. Seeing how I never slept the night with any hoes, because I left after the fucking was over, I didn't know how to play this out. She was my girl, I loved her and wanted to be with her, so I wanted to get to the heart of the matter.

"Are we good, bae? You gon' take me back?" I rubbed my hands up and down her back.

"Yes, we're good." The tension drained from her and her shoulders slumped in relief. "I thought you would change your mind and I was just preparing myself."

"After all that begging I did? Hell nah, I ain't change my mind." Even though I told her I didn't think I could be with her after she slept with that nigga, I just needed some time to cool off.

"Well, breakfast is almost ready. You want to get Keira up?"

I rubbed her booty and pulled her closer. "I'll get her up as long as you promise me my bacon won't be burned and my eggs ain't runny." We both chuckled at the reminder of how she did me when she was mad at me.

"I guess you have to trust me and find out," she said with a playful expression on her face.

"I trust you with my life," I told her seriously.

The expression on her face quickly changed, letting me know my early morning teasing had just turned serious.

"I am not so naïve like I used to be. Shit is going to change around here. You better get your business things in order so it doesn't take so much of your time." She stepped back and folded her arms over her chest, daring me to naysay her. "None of that previous shit you fucking pulled gon' fly around here. I want all of you or none of you, so *don't fuck with my heart.*"

Shaunie had always been feisty when angry. However, I noticed a little hardness in her that only pain and experiences leave on a woman. I pulled her to me and kissed her pouting lips. When I pulled back, I stared in her eyes, so she could see my sincerity, love, and regret.

"I swear to do right by you. I love you and just need another chance to prove it." She nodded her head, while keeping eye contact with me.

"Okay." She kissed my lips and turned away, back to the stove. "Breakfast is ready. Go and get your daughter."

I walked out of the kitchen feeling like a king. I'd be damned if I let my queen get away. Everything was falling into place. My family was back together and I had a chance to be the man I should have long been for them. It was a matter of time before my business affairs got back in line, too.

***

Thursday night rolled around and I was hyped. I knew the rat was gon' take the bait, so I had Rayne, Thugga, and Hassan riding with me for this one. My young hittas were across town at the location that the shooter gave me at the warehouse. They were instructed to kill any and everything moving.

We were camped out outside of the house where the keys were. Dressed in all black, with bulletproof vests and silencers on our guns, we were strategically placed around the house. Thugga and Hassan was covering the back and me and Rayne covered the front.

After waiting forty-five minutes and until it was almost pitch black in the neighborhood, an unknown car pulled up and parked a few houses down from the house we sometimes used for meetings. No one got out of the car immediately and I wasn't sure they weren't visiting a neighboring house. Taking out my phone, I sent a quick text to Thugga to let him know we had company and to keep his guard up. I was worried about sounds or lighting from the phone giving our locations away, so we all turned off the volume and adjusted the phone screen to the dimmest setting.

Eventually, the driver got out of the car with a crow bar. His face was covered in a ski mask and he wore a hoodie, so I couldn't tell who it could possibly be. I watched as he walked up to the house and kicked the door repeatedly until it gave in.

Once he was inside, Rayne and I ran across the street. With my trigger finger ready, I checked the car and was surprised to find it empty. *How you gon' hit a spot and don't have no back up?* I thought.

Moving away from the car, we used the night to shadow our approach to the house. The few pieces of furniture that was inside the house was turned over. Rayne check the other rooms as I silently crept upstairs. I heard rumbling in one of the rooms as I took the stairs. Just when I placed my foot on the fourth stair, it creaked and the noise stopped. Fuck! Not wanting to alert the would be robber that we were in the house, I stood still. When I heard footsteps coming towards the stairs, I started moving backwards. I had my vest on, but could still take a head shot.

Pow! Pow! Pow! Pow! Pow! Just when my feet touched the bottom of the stairs, several bullets flew near my head and body.

"Uuuuurrrrghhhh. Fuck!" I said in a voice barely above a whisper. The impact of the bullet felt like I was hit with a baseball bat. Checking off the shock of getting hit, I took cover behind the sofa and returned fire. Rayne, Hassan, and Thugga ran into the room and took cover. "I'm good." A burning sensation stung my chest, but I took a deep breath and pushed it back. "Rayne and Hassan, go outside in case that nigga try to jump out the window."

Rayne and Hassan nodded and eased back out the room. At the sound of their footsteps, more bullets rained in the room, followed by a body that stood at the top of the stairs.

Pht! Pht! Pht! Pht! Thugga and I returned fire, but the traitor had the cover of the stairs landing.

"Nigga, the jig is up. I know yo bitch ass is behind all this bullshit with my spots. Face me like a G and stop all this backstabbing. Leave that shit for the bitches."

Pht! Pht! Pht! He didn't respond and I saved my bullets. We were at an impasse, but he wasn't leaving there alive. Thugga held up his hand with his index and middle finger, mimicking walking. I nodded my head, signaling him to do it. He moved from his spot and feigned like he was going to hit the stairs, but quickly took cover.

Pow! Pow! Pow! Click. My fucking heart soared when I heard the click of an empty magazine. I didn't want to be surprised by more bullets. All my niggas carried more than one gun. When I heard footsteps retreating from the top of the landing, I took off for the stairs, followed by Thugga.

I made it to the top and headed in the direction of the noise. From the hall, I saw the door was open and the figure trying to pry the window open.

"You may as well stop. You ain't leaving this motherfucker. At least not alive anyway."

He stilled at the window, but didn't turn around. With vigor, he continued to try to open the jammed window. At the same time I fully entered the room, he got the window to open. Before he could climb out, I shot him twice in the back and he slumped over.

Thugga entered the room and saw the person on the floor with blood leaking from bullet holes.

"Fuck man, who is it?"

"Let's fucking find out." With my gun aimed at the figure, I approached slowly. When I got within three feet of him, I put my hand out and turned him over. The rapid rise and fall of his chest told me he was still alive. Gripping the ski mask, I pulled it from over his face and revealed the person who used to sit at my table and break bread. The nigga I grew up with. My teeth grinded together, because my jaws were snapped closed tight in anger.

I finally had the answer to who had been betraying me. With narrowed eyes, I said, "Nigga, you know how the fuck I get down. My circle is small, I'm loyal to my crew to the end, and you should know to never fuck me over." I trained my gun on him and pulled the trigger.

To Be Continued...
These Niggas Ain't Loyal 3
Coming Soon

Coming Soon From Lock Down Publications

GANGSTA CITY

By **Teddy Duke**

A DANGEROUS LOVE **VII**

By **J Peach**

LOVE KNOWS NO BOUNDARIES **III**

By **Coffee**

BURY ME A G **III**

By **Tranay Adams**

BLOOD OF A BOSS **III**

By **Askari**

DON'T FU#K WITH MY HEART **III**

By **Linnea**

THE KING CARTEL **II**

By **Frank Gresham**

SILVER PLATTER HOE **II**

By **Reds Johnson**

THESE NIGGAS AIN'T LOYAL **III**

By **Nikki Tee**

BROOKLYN ON LOCK

By **Sonovia Alexander**

THESE STREETS BLEED MURDER

By **Jerry Jackson**

DIRTY LICKS

By **Peter Mack**

ULTIMATE BETRAYAL

By **Phoenix**

CONFESSIONS OF A DOPEMAN'S DAUGHTER

By **Rasstrina**

Available Now

LOVE KNOWS NO BOUNDARIES **I & II**

By **Coffee**

SLEEPING IN HEAVEN, WAKING IN HELL **I, II & III**

By **Forever Redd**

THE DEVIL WEARS TIMBS **I, II & III**

By **Tranay Adams**

DON'T FU#K WITH MY HEART **I & II**

By **Linnea**

BOSS'N UP **I & II**

By **Royal Nicole**

A DANGEROUS LOVE **I, II, III, IV, V, VI**

By **J Peach**

CUM FOR ME

An **LDP Erotica Collaboration**

THE KING CARTEL

By **Frank Gresham**

BLOOD OF A BOSS **I & II**

By **Askari**

STREET JUSTICE

By **Chance**

BURY ME A G **I & II**

By **Tranay Adams**

BONDS OF DECEPTION

By **Lady Stiletto**

LOYALTY IS BLIND

By **Kenneth Chisholm**

A HUSTLA'Z AMBITION

By **Damion King**

THESE NIGGAS AIN'T LOYAL

By **Nikki Tee**

BOOKS BY LDP'S CEO, CA$H

TRUST NO MAN

TRUST NO MAN 2

TRUST NO MAN 3

BONDED BY BLOOD

SHORTY GOT A THUG

A DIRTY SOUTH LOVE

THUGS CRY

THUGS CRY 2

TRUST NO BITCH

TRUST NO BITCH 2

TRUST NO BITCH 3

TIL MY CASKET DROPS

Coming Soon

TRUST NO BITCH (EYEZ' STORY)

THUGS CRY 3

BONDED BY BLOOD 2

These Niggas Ain't Loyal 2